Meeting Leo Valent

Eliza had known all along their fling couldn't go anywhere, but she had lived each day as if it could and would. Leo Valente wasn't just charming, but ruthlessly, stubbornly and irresistibly determined with it. As each day passed she had fallen more and more in love with him. She had been like a starving person encountering their first feast. She had gobbled up every moment she could with him and to hell with the consequences.

"I have another proposal for you," he said now.

Eliza swallowed tightly and hoped he hadn't seen it. "Not marriage, I hope."

He laughed but it wasn't a nice sound. "Not marriage, no," he said. "A business proposal—a very lucrative one."

Eliza tried to read his expression. There was something in his dark brown eyes that was slightly menacing. Her heart beat a little bit faster as fear climbed up her spine with icy cold fingers. "What are you offering?"

"Five hundred thousand pounds. On the condition you spend the next month with me in Italy."

All about the author...
Melanie Milburne

From as soon as **MELANIE MILBURNE** could pick up a pen she knew she wanted to write. It was when she picked up her first Harlequin Mills and Boon at seventeen that she realized she wanted to write romance. Distracted for a few years by meeting and marrying her own handsome hero, surgeon husband Steve, and having two boys, plus completing a master's of education and becoming a nationally ranked athlete (masters swimming), she decided to write. Five submissions later she sold her first book and is now a multipublished, award-winning, *USA TODAY* bestselling author. In 2008 she won the Australian Romance Readers Association's most popular category/series romance and in 2011 she won the prestigious Romance Writers of Australia R*BY award.

Melanie loves to hear from her readers via her website, www.melaniemilburne.com.au, or on Facebook.

Other titles by Melanie Milburne available in ebook:

Harlequin Presents®

DESERVING OF HIS DIAMONDS
(The Outrageous Sisters)
ENEMIES AT THE ALTAR
(The Outrageous Sisters)
SURRENDERING ALL BUT HER HEART
UNCOVERING THE SILVERI SECRET

Melanie Milburne

HIS FINAL BARGAIN

Recycling programs for this product may not exist in your area.

ISBN-13: 978-0-373-13153-2

HIS FINAL BARGAIN

This edition published by arrangement with Harlequin Books S.A.

For questions and comments about the quality of this book, please contact us at CustomerService@Harlequin.com.

HARLEQUIN®
TM www.Harlequin.com

Printed in U.S.A.

HIS FINAL BARGAIN

With special thanks to Rose
at The Royal Guide Dogs of Tasmania
for her time in helping me research this novel.

Also special thanks to Josie Caporetto and
Serena Tatti for their help with Italian phrases.
Thanks to you all!

CHAPTER ONE

IT WAS THE meeting Eliza had been anticipating with agonising dread for weeks. She took her place with the four other teachers in the staffroom and prepared herself for the announcement from the headmistress.

'We're closing.'

The words fell into the room like the drop of a guillotine. The silence that followed echoed with a collective sense of disappointment, despair and panic. Eliza thought of her little primary school pupils with their sad and neglected backgrounds so similar to her own. She had worked so hard to get them to where they were now. What would happen to them if their small community-based school was shut down? They already had so much going against them, coming from such underprivileged backgrounds. They would never survive in the overcrowded mainstream school system. They would slip between the cracks, just like their parents and grandparents had done.

Like she had almost done.

The heartbreaking cycle of poverty and neglect would continue. Their lives—those little lives that had so much potential—would be stymied, ruined, and possibly even destroyed by delinquency and crime.

'Is there nothing we can do to keep things going for

a little while at least?' Georgie Brant, the Year Three teacher asked. 'What about another bake sale or a fair?'

The headmistress, Marcia Gordon, shook her head sadly. 'I'm afraid no amount of cakes and cookies are going to keep us afloat at this stage. We need a large injection of funds and we need it before the end of term.'

'But that's only a week away!' Eliza said.

Marcia sighed. 'I know. I'm sorry but that's just the way it is. We've always tried to keep our overheads low, but with the economy the way it is just now it's made it so much harder. We have no other choice but to close before we amass any more debt.'

'What if some of us take a pay cut or even work without pay?' Eliza suggested. 'I could go without pay for a month or two.' Any longer than that and things would get pretty dire. But she couldn't bear to stand back and do nothing. Surely there was something they could do? Surely there was someone they could appeal to for help…a charity or a government grant.

Something—*anything*.

Before Eliza could form the words Georgie had leaned forward in her chair and spoke them for her. 'What if we appeal for public support? Remember all the attention we got when Lizzie was given that teaching award last year? Maybe we could do another press article showing what we offer here for disadvantaged kids. Maybe some filthy-rich philanthropist will step out of the woodwork and offer to keep us going.' She rolled her eyes and slumped back in her seat dejectedly. 'Of course, it would help if one of us actually knew someone filthy-rich.'

Eliza sat very still in her seat. The hairs on the back of her neck each stood up one by one and began tingling at the roots. A fine shiver moved over her skin like the rush of a cool breeze. Every time she thought of Leo Valente her body reacted as if he was in the room with her. Her heart picked up its pace as she brought those darkly handsome features to mind…

'Do *you* know anyone, Lizzie?' Georgie asked, turning towards her.

'Um…no,' Eliza said. 'I don't mix in those sorts of circles.' *Any more.*

Marcia clicked her pen on and off a couple of times, her expression thoughtful. 'I suppose it wouldn't hurt to try. I'll make a brief statement to the press. Even if we could stay open until Christmas it would be something.' She stood up and gathered her papers off the table. 'I'm sending the letter to the parents in tomorrow's post.' She sighed again. 'For those of you who believe in miracles, now is a good time to pray for one.'

Eliza saw the car as soon as she turned the corner into her street. It was prowling slowly like a black panther on the hunt, its halogen headlights beaming like searching eyes. It was too dark inside the car to see the driver in any detail, but she immediately sensed it was a man and that it was her he was looking for. A telltale shiver passed over her like the hand of a ghost as the driver expertly guided the showroom-perfect Mercedes into the only available car space outside her flat.

Her breath stalled in her throat as a tall, dark-haired, well dressed figure got out from behind the wheel. Her heart jolted against her ribcage and her pulse quickened. Seeing Leo Valente face to face for the first time in four years created a shockwave through her body that left her feeling disoriented and dizzy. Even her legs felt shaky as if the ground beneath her had suddenly turned to jelly.

Why was he here? What did he want? How had he found her?

She strove for a steady composure as he came to stand in front of her on the pavement, but inside her stomach was fluttering like a moth trapped in a jam jar. 'Leo,' she said, surprised her voice came out at all with her throat so tightly constricted with emotion.

He inclined his darkly handsome head in a formal greeting. 'Eliza.'

She quickly disguised a swallow. His voice, with its sexy Italian accent, had always made her go weak at the knees. His looks were just as lethally attractive—tall and lean and arrestingly handsome, with eyes so dark a brown they looked almost black. The landscape of his face hinted at a man who was used to getting his own way. It was there in the chiselled line of his jaw and the uncompromising set to his mouth. He looked a little older than when she had last seen him. His jet-black hair had a trace of silver at the temples, and there were fine lines grooved either side of his mouth and around his eyes, which somehow she didn't think smiling or laughter had caused.

'Hi…' she said and then wished she had gone for something a little more formal. It wasn't as if they had parted as friends—far from it.

'I would like to speak to you in private.' He nodded towards her ground-floor flat, the look in his eyes determined, intractable and diamond-hard. 'Shall we go inside?'

She took an uneven breath that rattled against her throat. 'Um…I'm kind of busy right now…'

His eyes hardened even further as if he knew it for the lie it was. 'I won't take any more than five or ten minutes of your time.'

Eliza endured the silent tug-of-war between his gaze and hers for as long as she could, but in the end she was the first to look away. 'All right.' She blew out a little gust of a breath. 'Five minutes.'

She was aware of him walking behind her up the cracked and uneven pathway to her front door. She tried not to fumble with her keys but the way they rattled and jingled in her fingers betrayed her nervousness lamentably. Finally she got the door open and stepped through, inwardly cringing when she thought of how humble her little flat was compared to his villa in Positano. She could only imagine what he was thinking: *How could she have settled for this instead of what I offered her?*

Eliza turned to face him as he came in. He had to stoop to enter, his broad shoulders almost spanning the narrow hallway. He glanced around with a critical eye. Was he wondering if the ceiling was going to come tumbling down on him? She watched as his top lip developed a slight curl as he turned back to face her. 'How long have you lived here?'

Pride brought her chin up half an inch. 'Four years.'

'You're renting?'

Eliza silently ground her teeth. Was he doing it deliberately? Reminding her of all she had thrown away by rejecting his proposal of marriage? He must know she could never afford to buy in this part of London. She couldn't afford to buy in *any* part of London. And now with her job hanging in the balance she might not even be able to afford to pay her rent. 'I'm saving up for a place of my own,' she said as she placed her bag on the little hall table.

'I might be able to help you with that.'

She searched his expression but it was hard to know what was going on behind the dark screen of his eyes.

She quickly moistened her lips, trying to act nonchalant in spite of that little butterfly in her stomach, which had suddenly developed razor blades for wings. 'I'm not sure what you're suggesting,' she said. 'But just for the record—thanks but no thanks.'

His eyes tussled with hers again. 'Is there somewhere we can talk other than out here in the hall?'

Eliza hesitated as she did a quick mental survey of her tiny sitting room. She had been sorting through a stack of magazines one of the local newsagents had given her for craftwork with her primary school class yesterday. Had she closed that gossip magazine she had been reading? Leo had been photographed at some charity function in Rome. The magazine was a couple of weeks old but it was the only time she had seen anything of him in the press. He had always fiercely guarded his private life. Seeing his photo so soon after the staff meeting had unsettled her deeply. She had stared and stared at his image, wondering if it was just a coincidence that he had appeared like that, seemingly from out of nowhere. 'Um…sure,' she said. 'Come this way.'

If Leo had made the hallway seem small, he made the sitting room look like something out of a Lilliputian house. She grimaced as his head bumped the cheap lantern light fitting. 'You'd better sit down,' she said, surreptitiously closing the magazine and putting it beneath the others in the stack. 'You have the sofa.'

'Where are you going to sit?' he asked with a crook of one dark brow.

'Um…I'll get a chair from the kitchen…'

'I'll get it,' he said. 'You take the sofa.'

Eliza would have argued over it except for the fact that her legs weren't feeling too stable right at that moment. She sat on the sofa and placed her hands flat on her thighs to stop them from trembling. He placed the chair in what little space was left in front of the sofa and sat down in a classically dominant pose with his hands resting casually on his widely set apart strongly muscled thighs.

She waited for him to speak. The silence seemed endless as he sat there quietly surveying her with that dark inscrutable gaze.

'You're not wearing a wedding ring,' he said.

'No…' She clasped her hands together in her lap, her cheeks feeling as if she had been sitting too close to a fire.

'But you're still engaged.'

Eliza sought the awkward bump of the solitaire diamond with her fingers. 'Yes…yes, I am…'

His eyes burned as they held hers, with resentment, with hatred. 'Rather a long betrothal, is it not?' he said. 'I'm surprised your fiancé is so patient.'

She thought of poor broken Ewan, strapped in that chair with his vacant stare, day after day, year after year, dependent on others for everything. Yes, patient was exactly what Ewan was now. 'He seems content with the arrangement as it stands,' she said.

A tiny muscle flickered beneath his skin in the lower quadrant of his jaw. 'And what about you?' he asked with a pointed look that seemed to burn right through to her backbone. 'Are *you* content?'

Eliza forced herself to hold his penetrating gaze. Would he be able to see how lonely and miserable she was? How *trapped* she was? 'I'm perfectly happy,' she said, keeping her expression under rigidly tight control.

'Does he live here with you?'

'No, he has his own place.'

'Then why don't you share it with him?'

Eliza shifted her gaze to look down at her clasped hands. She noticed she had blue poster paint under one of her fingernails and a smear of yellow on the back of one knuckle. She absently rubbed at the smear with the pad of her thumb. 'It's a bit far for me to travel each day to school,' she said. 'We spend the weekends together whenever we can.'

The silence was long and brooding—*angry*.

She looked up when she heard the rustle of his clothes as he got to his feet. He prowled about the room like a tiger shark in a goldfish bowl. His hands were tightly clenched, but every now and again he would open them and loosen his fingers before fisting them again.

He suddenly stopped pacing and nailed her with his hard, embittered gaze. 'Why?'

Eliza affected a coolly composed stance. 'Why… what?'

His eyes blazed with hatred. 'Why did you choose him over me?'

'I met him first and he loves me.' She had often wondered how different her life would have been if she hadn't met Ewan. Would it have been better or worse? It was hard to say. There had been so many good times before the accident.

His brows slammed together. 'You think I didn't?'

Eliza let out a little breath of scorn. 'You didn't love me, Leo. You were in love with the idea of settling down because you'd just lost your father. I was the first one who came along who fitted your checklist—young, biddable and beddable.'

'I could've given you anything money can buy,' he said through tight lips. 'And yet you choose to live like a pauper while tied to a man who doesn't even have the desire to live with you full-time. How do you know he's not cheating on you while you're here?'

'I can assure you he's not cheating on me,' Eliza said with sad irony. She knew exactly where Ewan was and who he was with twenty-four hours a day, seven days a week.

'Do you cheat on him?' he asked with a cynical look.

She pressed her lips together without answering.

His expression was dark with anger. 'Why didn't you tell me right from the start? You should have told me you were engaged the first time we met. Why wait until I proposed to you to tell me you were promised to another man?'

Eliza thought back to those three blissful weeks in Italy four years ago. It had been her first holiday since Ewan's accident eighteen months before. His mother Samantha had insisted she get away for a break.

Eliza had gone without her engagement ring; one of the claws had needed repairing so she had left it with the jeweller while she was away. For those few short weeks she had tried to be just like any other single girl, knowing that when she got back the prison doors would close on her for good.

Meeting Leo Valente had been so bittersweet. She had known all along their fling couldn't go anywhere, but she had lived each day as if it could and would. She had been swept up in the romantic excitement of it, pretending to herself that it wasn't doing anyone any harm if she had those few precious weeks pretending she was free. She had not intended to fall in love with him. But she had seriously underestimated Leo Valente. He wasn't just charming, but ruthlessly, stubbornly and irresistibly determined with it. She had found herself enraptured by his intellectually stimulating company and by his intensely passionate lovemaking.

As each day passed she had fallen more and more in love with him. The clock had been ticking on their time together but she hadn't been able to stop herself from seeing him. She had been like a starving person encountering their first feast. She had gobbled up every moment she could with him and to hell with the consequences.

'In hindsight I agree with you,' Eliza said. 'I probably should've said something. But I thought it was just a holiday fling. I didn't expect to ever see you again. I certainly didn't expect you to propose to me. We'd only known each other less than a month.'

His expression pulsed again with bitterness. 'Did you have a good laugh about it with your friends when you came home? Is that why you let me make a fool of myself, just so you could dine out on it ever since?'

Eliza got to her feet and wrapped her arms around her body as if she were cold, even though the flat was stuffy from being closed up all day. She went over to the window and looked at the solitary rose bush in the front garden. It had a single bloom on it but the rain and the wind had assaulted its velvet petals until only three were left clinging precariously to the craggy, thorny stem. 'I didn't tell anyone about it,' she said. 'When I came back home it felt like it had all been a dream.'

'Did you tell your fiancé about us?'

'No.'

'Why not?'

She grasped her elbows a bit tighter and turned to face him. 'He wouldn't have understood.'

'I bet he wouldn't.' He gave a little sound of disdain. 'His fiancée opens her legs for the first man she meets in a bar while on holiday. Yes, I would imagine he would find that rather hard to understand.'

Eliza gave him a glacial look. 'I think it might be time for you to leave. Your five minutes is up.'

He closed the distance between them in one stride. He towered over her, making her breath stall again in her chest. She saw his nostrils flare as if he was taking in her scent. She could smell his: a complex mix of wood and citrus and spice that tantalised her senses and stirred up a host of memories she had tried for so long to suppress. She felt her blood start to thunder through the network of her veins. She felt her skin tighten and tingle with awareness. She felt her insides coil and flex with a powerful stirring of lust. Her body recognised the intimate chemistry of his. It was as if she was finely tuned to his radar. No other man made her so aware of her body, so acutely aware of her primal reaction to him.

'I have another proposal for you,' he said.

Eliza swallowed tightly and hoped he hadn't seen it. 'Not marriage, I hope.'

He laughed but it wasn't a nice sound. 'Not marriage, no,' he said. 'A business proposal—a very lucrative one.'

Eliza tried to read his expression. There was something in his dark brown eyes that was slightly menacing. Her heart beat a little bit faster as fear climbed up her spine with icy-cold fingers. 'I don't want or need your money,' she said with a flash of stubborn pride.

His top lip gave a sardonic curl. 'Perhaps not, but your cash-strapped community school does.'

She desperately tried to conceal her shock. How on earth did he know? The press article hadn't even gone to press. The journalist and photographer had only just left the school a couple of hours ago. How had he found out about it so quickly? Had he done his *own* research? What else had he uncovered about her? She gave him a wary look. 'What are you offering?'

'Five hundred thousand pounds.'

Her eyes widened. 'On what condition?'

His eyes glinted dangerously. 'On the condition you spend the next month with me in Italy.'

Eliza felt her heart drop like an anchor. She moistened her lips, struggling to maintain her outwardly calm composure when everything inside her was in a frenzied turmoil. 'In…in what capacity?'

'I need a nanny.'

A pain sliced through the middle of her heart like the slash of a scimitar. 'You're…*married?*'

His eyes remained cold and hard, his mouth a grim flat line. 'Widowed,' he said. 'I have a daughter. She's three.'

Eliza mentally did the sums. He must have met his wife not long after she left Italy. For some reason that hurt much more than if his marriage had been a more recent thing. He had moved on with his life so quickly. No long, lonely months of pining for her, of not eating and not sleeping. No. He had forgotten all about her, while she had never forgotten him, not even for a day. But there had been nothing in the press about him marrying or even about his wife dying. Who was she? What had happened to her? Should she ask?

Eliza glanced at his left hand. 'You're not wearing a wedding ring.'

'No.'

'What…um—happened?'

His eyes continued to brutalise hers with their dark brooding intensity. 'To my wife?'

Eliza nodded. She felt sick with anguish hearing him

say those words. *My wife.* Those words had been meant for *her*, not someone else. She couldn't bear to think of him with someone else, making love with someone else, *loving* someone else. She had taught herself *not* to think about it. It was too painful to imagine the life she might have had with him if things had been different.

If she had been free...

'Giulia killed herself.' He said the words without any trace of emotion. He might have been reading the evening news, so indifferent was his tone. And yet something about his expression—that flicker of pain that came and went in his eyes—hinted that his wife's death had been a shattering blow to him.

'I'm very sorry,' Eliza said. 'How devastating that must have been…must still be…'

'It has been very difficult for my daughter,' he said. 'She doesn't understand why her mother is no longer around.'

Eliza understood all too well the utter despair little children felt when a parent died or deserted them. She had been just seven years old when her mother had left her with distant relatives to go on a drugs and drinking binge that had ended in her death. But it had been months and months before her great-aunt had told her that her mother wasn't coming back to collect her. She hadn't even been taken to the graveside to say a proper goodbye. 'Have you explained to your daughter that her mother has passed away?' she asked.

'Alessandra is only three years old.'

'That doesn't mean she won't be able to understand what's happened,' she said. 'It's important to be truthful with her, not harshly or insensitively, but compassionately. Little children understand much more than we give them credit for.'

He moved to the other side of the room, standing with his back to her as he looked at the street outside. It seemed a long time before he spoke. 'Alessandra is not like other little children.'

Eliza moistened her parchment-dry lips. 'Look—I'm not sure if I'm the right person to help you. I work full-time as a primary school teacher. I have commitments and responsibilities to see to. I can't just up and leave the country for four weeks.'

He turned back around and pinned her with his gaze. 'Without my help you won't even have a job. Your school is about to be shut down.'

She frowned at him. 'How do you know that? How can you possibly know that? There's been nothing in the press so far.'

'I have my contacts.'

He had definitely done his research, Eliza thought. Who had he been talking to? She knew he was a powerful man, but it made her uneasy to think he had found out so much about her situation. What else had he found out?

'The summer holidays begin this weekend,' he said. 'You have six weeks to do what you like.'

'I've made other plans for the holidays. I don't want to change them at the last minute.'

He hooked one dark brow upwards. 'Not even for half a million pounds?'

Eliza pictured the money, great big piles of it. More money than she had ever seen. Money that would give her little primary school children the educational boost they so desperately needed to get out of the cycle of poverty they had been born into. But a month was a long time to spend with a man who was little more than a stranger to her now. What did he want from her? What would he want her to do? Was this some sort of payback or revenge attempt? How could she know what was behind his offer? He said he wanted a nanny, but what if he wanted more?

What if he wanted *her*?

'Why me?'

His inscrutable eyes gave nothing away. 'You have the qualifications I require for the post.'

It was Eliza's turn to arch an eyebrow. 'I just bet I do. Young and female with a pulse, correct?'

A glint of something dark and mocking entered his gaze as it held hers. 'You misunderstand me, Eliza. I am not offering you a rerun at being my mistress. You will be employed as my daughter's nanny. That is all that will be required of you.'

Why was she feeling as if he had just insulted her? What right did she have to bristle at his words? He needed a nanny. He didn't want her in any other capacity.

He didn't want her.

The realisation pained Eliza much more than she wanted it to. What foolish part of her had clung to the idea that even after all this time he would come back for her because he had never found anyone who filled the gaping hole she had left in his life? 'I can assure you that if you were offering me anything else I wouldn't accept it,' she said with a little hitch of her chin.

His gaze held hers in an assessing manner. It was unnerving to be subjected to such an intensely probing look, especially as she wasn't entirely confident she was keeping her reaction to him concealed. 'I wonder if that is strictly true,' he mused. 'Clearly your fiancé isn't satisfying you. You still have that hungry look about you.'

'You're mistaken,' she said with prickly defensiveness. 'You're seeing what you want to see, not what is.' *You're seeing what I'm trying so hard to hide!*

His dark brown eyes continued to impale hers. 'Will you accept the post?'

Eliza caught at her lower lip for a brief moment. She had at her fingertips the way to keep the school open. All of her children could continue with their education. The parenting and counselling programme for single mums she had dreamt of offering could very well become a reality if there were more funds available—a programme that might have saved her mother if it had been available at the time.

'Will another five hundred thousand pounds in cash help you come to a decision a little sooner?'

Eliza gaped at him. Was he really offering her a million pounds in cash? Did people *do* that? Were there really people out there who *could* do that?

She had grown up with next to nothing, shunted from place to place while her mother continued on a wretched cycle of drug and alcohol abuse that was her way of self-medicating far deeper emotional issues that had their origin in childhood. Eliza wasn't used to having enough money for the necessities, let alone the luxuries. As a child she had dreamt of having enough money to get her mother the help she so desperately needed, but there hadn't been enough for food and rent at times, let alone therapy.

She knew she came from a very different background from Leo, but he had never flaunted his wealth in the past. She had thought him surprisingly modest about it considering he was a self-made man. Thirty years ago his father had lost everything in a business deal gone sour. Leo had worked long and hard to rebuild the family engineering company from scratch. And he had done it and done it well. The Valente Engineering Company was responsible for some of the biggest projects across the globe. She had admired him for turning things around. So many people would have given up or adopted a victim mentality but he had not.

But for all the wealth Leo Valente had, it certainly hadn't bought him happiness. Eliza could see the lines of strain on his face and the shadows in his eyes that hadn't been there four years ago. She sent her tongue out over her lips again. 'Cash?'

He gave a businesslike nod. 'Cash. But only if you sign up right here and now.'

She frowned. 'You want me to sign something?'

He took out a folded sheet of paper from the inside of his jacket without once breaking his gaze lock with hers. 'A confidentiality agreement. No press interviews before, during or once your appointment is over.'

Eliza took the document and glanced over it. It was reasonably straightforward. She was forbidden to speak to the press, otherwise she would have to repay the amount he was giving her with twenty per cent interest. She looked up at him again. 'You certainly put a very high price on your privacy.'

'I have seen lives and reputations destroyed by idle speculation in the press,' he said. 'I will not tolerate any scurrilous rumour mongering. If you don't think you can abide by the rules set out in that document, then I will leave now and let you get on with your life. There will be no need for any further contact between us.'

Eliza couldn't help wondering why he wanted contact with her now. Why her? He could afford to employ the most highly qualified nanny in the world.

They hadn't parted on the best of terms. Every time she thought of that final scene between them she felt sick to her stomach. He had been livid to find out she was already engaged to another man. His anger had been palpable. She had felt bruised by it even though he had only touched her with his gaze. Oh, those hard, bitter eyes! How they had stabbed and burned her with their hatred and loathing. He hadn't even given her time to explain. He had stormed out of the restaurant and out of her life. He had cut all contact with her.

She could so easily have defended herself back then and in the weeks and months and years since. At any one point she could have called him and told him. She could have explained it all, but guilt had kept her silent.

It still kept her silent.

Dare she go with him? For a million pounds how could she not? Strictly speaking, the money wasn't for her. That made it more palatable, or at least slightly. She would be doing it for the children and their poor disadvantaged mothers. It was only for a month. That wasn't a long time by anyone's standards. It would be over in a flash. Besides, England's summer was turning out to be a non-event. A month's break looking after a little girl in sun-drenched Positano would be a piece of cake.

How hard could it be?

Eliza straightened her spine and looked him in the eye as she held out her hand. 'Do you have a pen?'

CHAPTER TWO

LEO WATCHED AS Eliza scratched her signature across the paper. She had a neat hand, loopy and very feminine. He had loved those soft little hands on his body. His flesh had sung with delight every time she had touched him…

He jerked his thoughts back like a rider tugging the reins on a bolting horse. He would *not* allow himself to think of her that way. He needed a nanny. This was strictly a business arrangement. There was nothing else he wanted from her.

Four years on he was still furious with her for what she had done. He was even more furious with himself for falling for her when she had only been using him. How had he been so beguiled by her? She had reeled him in like a dumb fish on a line. She had dangled the bait and he had gobbled it up without thinking of what he was doing. He had acted like a lovesick swain by proposing to her so quickly. He had offered her the world—his world, the one he had worked such back-breaking hours to make up from scratch.

She had captivated him from the moment she had taken the seat beside him in the bar where he had been sitting brooding into his drink on the night of his father's funeral. There was a restless sort of energy about her that he had recognised and responded to instantly.

He had felt his body start to sizzle as soon as her arm brushed against his. She had been upfront and brazen with him, but in an edgy, exhilarating way. Their first night together had been monumentally explosive. He had never felt such a maelstrom of lust. He had been totally consumed by it. He had taken what he could with her, how he could, relishing that she seemed to want to do the same. He had loved that about her, that her need for him was as lusty and racy as his for her.

Their one-night stand had morphed into a passionate three-week affair that had him issuing a romantic proposal because he couldn't bear the thought of never seeing her again. But all that time she had been harbouring a secret—she was already engaged to a man back home in England.

Leo looked at her left hand. Her engagement ring glinted at him, taunting him like an evil eye.

Anger was like a red mist in front of him. He had been nothing more to her than a holiday fling, a diversion—a shallow little hook-up to laugh about with her friends once she got home.

He *hated* her for it.

He hated her for how his life had turned out since.

The life he'd planned for himself had been derailed by her betrayal. It had had a domino effect on every part of his life since. If it hadn't been for her perfidy he would not have met poor, sad, lonely Giulia. The guilt he felt about Giulia's death was like a clamp around his heart. He had been the wrong person for her. She had been the wrong person for him. But in their mutual despair over being let down by the ones they had loved, they had formed a wretched sort of alliance that was always going to end in tragedy. From the first moment Giulia had set eyes on their dark-haired baby girl she had rejected her. She had seemed repulsed by her own child. The doctors talked about post-natal depression and other failure to bond issues, given that the baby had been premature and had special needs, but deep inside Leo already knew what the problem had been.

Giulia hadn't wanted *his* child; she had wanted her ex's.

He had been a very poor substitute husband for her, but he was determined to be the best possible father he could be to his little daughter.

Bringing Eliza back into his life to help with Alessandra would be a way of putting things in order once and for all. Revenge was an ugly word. He didn't want to think along those lines. This was more of a way of drawing a line under that part of his life.

This time *he* would be in the driving seat. Once the month was up she could pack her bags and leave. It was a business arrangement, just like any other.

No feelings were involved.

Eliza handed him back his pen. 'I can't start until school finishes at the end of the week.'

Leo pocketed the pen, trying to ignore the warmth it had taken from her fingers. Trying to ignore the hot wave of lust that rumbled beneath his skin like a wild beast waking up after a long hibernation.

He *had* to ignore it.

He *would* ignore it.

'I understand that,' he said. 'I will send a car to take you to the airport on Friday. The flight has already been booked.'

Her blue-green eyes widened in surprise or affront, he couldn't be quite sure which. 'You're very certain of yourself, aren't you?'

'I'm used to getting what I want. I don't allow minor obstacles to get in my way.'

Her chin came up a notch and her eyes took on a glittering, challenging sheen. 'I don't think I've ever been described as a "minor obstacle" before. What if I turn out to be a much bigger challenge than you bargained for?'

Leo had already factored in the danger element. It was dangerous to have her back in his life. He knew that. But in a perverse sort of way he *wanted* that. He was sick of his pallid life. She represented all that he had lost—the colour, the vibrancy and the passion.

The energy.

He could feel it now, zinging along his veins like an electric pulse. *She* did that to him. She made him feel alive again. She had done that to him four years ago. He was aware of her in a way he had never felt with any other woman. She spoke to him on a visceral level. He felt the communication in his flesh, in *every* pore of his skin. He could feel it now, how his body stood to attention when she was near: the blood pulsing through his veins, the urgent need already thickening beneath his clothes.

Did she feel the same need too?

She was acting all cool and composed on the surface, but now and again he caught her tugging at her lower lip with her teeth and her gaze would fall away from his. Was she remembering how wanton she had been in his arms? How he had made her scream and thrash about as she came time and time again? His flesh tingled at the memory of her hot little body clutching at him so tightly. He had felt every rippling contraction of her orgasms. Was that how she responded to her fiancé? His gut roiled at the thought of her with that nameless, faceless man she had chosen over him. 'I think it's pretty safe to say I can handle whatever you dish up,' he said. 'I'm used to women like you. I know the games you like to play.'

The defiant gleam in her eyes made them seem more green than blue. 'If you find my company so distasteful then why are you employing me to look after your daughter?'

'You have a good reputation with handling small children,' Leo said. 'I was sitting in an airport gate lounge about a year ago when I happened to read an article in one of the papers about the work you do with unprivileged children. You were given an award for teaching excellence. I recognised your name. I thought there couldn't be two Eliza Lincolns working as primary school teachers in London. I assumed—quite rightly as it turns out—that it was you.'

Her look was more guarded now than defiant. 'I still don't understand why you want me to work for you, especially considering how things ended between us.'

'Alessandra's usual nanny has a family emergency to attend to,' he said. 'It's left me in a bit of a fix. I only need someone for the summer break. Kathleen will return at the end of August. You'll be back well in time for the resumption of school.'

'That still doesn't answer my question as to why me.'

Leo had only recently come to realise he was never going to be satisfied until he had drawn a line under his relationship with her. She'd had all the power the last time. This time he would take control and he would not relinquish it until he was satisfied that he could live the rest of his life without flinching whenever he thought of her. He didn't want another disastrous relationship—like the one he'd had with Giulia—because of the baggage he was carrying around. He wanted his life in order and the only way to do that was to deal with the past and put it to rest—*permanently*. 'At least I know what I'm getting with you,' he said. 'There will be no nasty surprises, *sì*?'

She arched a neatly groomed eyebrow. 'The devil you know?'

'Indeed.'

She hugged her arms around her body once more, her eyes moving out of the range of his. 'What are the arrangements as to my accommodation?'

'You will stay with us at my villa in Positano. I have a couple of developments I'm working on which may involve a trip abroad, either back here to London or Paris.'

Her gaze flicked back to his. 'Where is your daughter now? Is she here in London with you?'

Leo shook his head. 'No, she's with a fill-in girl from an agency. I'm keen to get back to make sure she's all right. She gets anxious around people she doesn't know.' He handed her his business card. 'Here are my contact details. I'll send a driver to collect you from the airport in Naples. I'll send half of the cash with an armoured guard in the next twenty-four hours. The rest I will deposit in your bank account if you give me your details.'

A little frown puckered her forehead. 'I don't think it's a good idea to bring that amount of money here. I'd rather you gave it straight to the school's bursar to deposit safely. I'll give you his contact details.'

'As you wish.' He pushed his sleeve back to check his watch. 'I have to go. I have one last meeting in the city before I fly back tonight. I'll see you when you get to my villa on Friday.'

She followed him to the door. 'What's your daughter's favourite colour?'

Leo's hand froze on the doorknob. He slowly turned and looked at her with a frown pulling at his brow. 'Why do you ask?'

'I thought I'd make her a toy. I knit them for the kids at school. They appreciate it being made for them specially. I make them in their favourite colour. Would she like a puppy or a teddy or a rabbit, do you think?'

Leo thought of his little daughter in her nursery at home, surrounded by hundreds of toys of every shape and size and colour. 'You choose.' He blew out a breath he hadn't realised he'd been holding. 'She's not fussy.'

Eliza watched as he strode back down the pathway to his car. He didn't look back at her before he drove off. It was as if he had dismissed her as soon as he walked out of her flat.

She looked at his business card in her hand. He had changed it since she had been with him four years ago. It was smoother, harder, more sophisticated.

Just like the man himself.

Why did he want her back in his life, even for a short time? It seemed a strange sort of request to ask an ex-lover to play nanny to his child by another woman. Was he doing it as an act of revenge? He couldn't possibly know how deeply painful she would find it.

She hadn't told him she loved him in the past. She had told him very little about herself. Their passionate time together had left little room for heart to heart outpourings. She had preferred it that way. The physicality of their relationship had been so different from anything else she had experienced before. Not that her experience was all that extensive given that she had been with Ewan since she was sixteen. She hadn't known any different until Leo had opened up a sensual paradise to her. He had made her body hum and tingle for hours. He had been able to do it just by looking at her.

He could still do it.

She took an unsteady breath as she thought about that dark gaze holding hers so forcefully. Had he seen how much he still affected her? He hadn't touched her. She had carefully avoided his fingers when he had handed her the paper and the pen and his card. But she had felt the warmth of where his fingers had been and her body had remembered every pulse-racing touch, as if he had flicked a switch to replay each and every erotic encounter in her brain. He had been a demanding lover, right from the word go, but then, so had she.

She had met him the evening of the day he had buried his father. He had been sitting in the bar of her hotel in Rome, taking an extraordinarily long time to drink a couple of fingers of whisky. She had been sitting in one of the leather chairs further back in the room, taking much less time working her way through a frightfully expensive cocktail she had ordered on impulse. She had felt in a reckless mood. It was her first night of freedom in so long. She was in a foreign country where no one knew who she was. That glimpse of freedom had been as heady and intoxicating as the drink she had bought. She had never in her life approached a man in a bar.

But that night was different.

Eliza had felt inexplicably drawn to him, like an iron filing being pulled into a powerful magnet's range. He fascinated her. Why was he sitting alone? Why was he taking forever to have one drink? He didn't look the type to be sitting by himself. He was far too good-looking for that. He was too well dressed. She wasn't one for being able to pick designer-wear off pat, but she was pretty sure his dark suit hadn't come off any department store rack in a marked down sale.

Eliza had walked over to him and slipped onto the bar stool right next to him. The skin of her bare arm had brushed against the fine cotton of his designer shirt. She could still remember the way her body had jolted as if she had touched a live source of power.

He had turned his head and locked gazes with her. It had sent another jolt through her body as that dark gaze meshed with hers. She had brazenly looked at his mouth, noting the sculptured definition of his top lip and the fuller, sinfully sensual contour of his lower one. He'd had a day's worth of stubble on his jaw. It had given him an aggressively masculine look that had made her blood simmer in her veins. She had looked down at his hand resting on the bar next to hers. His was so tanned and sprinkled with coarse masculine hair, the span of his fingers broad—man's hands, capable hands—clever hands. Her hand was so light and creamy, and her fingers so slim and feminine and small in comparison.

To this day she couldn't remember whose hand had touched whose first…

Thinking about that night in his hotel room still gave her shivers of delight. Her body had responded to his like bone-dry tinder did to a naked flame. She had erupted in his arms time and time again. It had been the most exciting, thrilling night of her life. She hadn't wanted it to end. She had thought that would be it—her first and only one-night stand. It would be something she would file away and occasionally revisit in her mind once she got back to her ordinary life. She had thought she would never see him again but she hadn't factored in his charm and determination. One night had turned into a three-week affair that had left her senses spinning and reeling. She knew it had been wrong not to tell him her tragic circumstances, but as each day passed it became harder and harder to say anything. She hadn't wanted to risk what little time she had left with him. So she had pushed it from her mind. Her life back in England was someone else's life. Another girl was engaged to poor broken Ewan—it wasn't her.

The day before she was meant to leave, Leo had taken her to a fabulous restaurant they had eaten in previously. He had booked a private room and had dozens of red roses delivered. Candles lit the room from every corner. Champagne was waiting in a beribboned silver ice bucket. A romantic ballad was playing in the background…

Eliza hastily backtracked out of her time travel. She hated thinking about that night; how she had foolishly deluded herself into thinking he'd been simply giving her a grand send-off to remember him by. Of course he had been doing no such thing. Halfway through the delicious meal he had presented her with a priceless-looking diamond. She had sat there staring at it for a long speechless moment.

And then she had looked into his eyes and said no.

'Have you heard the exciting news?' Georgie said as soon as Eliza got to school the following day. 'We're not closing. A rich benefactor has been found at the last minute. Can you believe it?'

Eliza put her bag in the drawer of her desk in the staffroom. 'That's wonderful.'

'You don't sound very surprised.'

'I am,' Eliza said, painting on a smile. 'I'm delighted. It's a miracle. It truly is.'

Georgie perched on the edge of the desk and swung her legs back and forth as if she was one of the seven-year-olds she taught. 'Marcia can't or won't say who it is. She said the donation was made anonymously. But who on earth hands over a million pounds like loose change?'

'Someone who has a lot of money, obviously.'

'Or an agenda.' Georgie tapped against her lips with a fingertip. 'I wonder who he is. It's got to be a he, hasn't it?'

'There are female billionaires in the world, you know.'

Georgie stopped swinging her legs and gave Eliza a pointed look. 'Do *you* know who it is?'

Eliza had spent most of her childhood masking her feelings. It was a skill she was rather grateful for now. 'How could I if the donation was made anonymously?'

'I guess you're right.' Georgie slipped off the desk as the bell rang. 'Are you heading down to Suffolk for the summer break?'

'Um…not this time. I've made other plans.'

Georgie's brows lifted. 'Where are you going?'

'Abroad.'

'Can you narrow that down a bit?'

'Italy.'

'Alone?'

'Yes and no,' Eliza said. 'It's kind of a busman's holiday. I'm filling in for a nanny who needs to take some leave.'

'It'll be good for you,' Georgie said. 'And it's not as if Ewan will mind either way, is it?'

'No…' Eliza let out a heavy sigh. 'He won't mind at all.'

CHAPTER THREE

WHEN ELIZA LANDED in Naples on Friday it wasn't a uniformed driver waiting to collect her but Leo himself. He greeted her formally as if she were indeed a newly hired nanny and not the woman he had once planned to spend the rest of his life with.

'How was your flight?' he asked as he picked up her suitcase.

'Fine, thank you.' She glanced around him. 'Is your daughter not with you?'

His expression became even more shuttered. 'She doesn't enjoy car travel. I thought it best to leave her with the agency girl. She'll be in bed by the time we get home. You can meet her properly tomorrow.'

Eliza followed him to where his car was parked. The warm air outside was like being enveloped in a thick, hot blanket. It had been dismally cold and rainy in London when she left, which had made her feel a little better about leaving, but not much.

She had phoned Ewan's mother about her change of plans. Samantha had been bitterly disappointed at first. She always looked forward to Eliza's visits. Eliza was aware of how Samantha looked upon her as a surrogate child now that Ewan was no longer able to fulfil her dreams as her son. But then, their relationship had always been friendly and companionable. She had found in Samantha Brockman the model of the mother she had always dreamed of having—someone who loved unconditionally, who wanted only the best for her child no matter how much it cost her, emotionally, physically or financially.

That was what had made it so terribly hard when she had decided to end things with Ewan. She knew it would be the end of any further contact with Samantha. She could hardly expect a mother to choose friendship over blood.

But then fate had made the choice for both of them.

Samantha still didn't know Eliza had broken her engagement to her son the night of his accident. How could she tell her that it was *her* fault Ewan had left her flat in such a state? The police said it was 'driver distraction' that caused the accident. The guilt Eliza felt was an ever-present weight inside her chest. Every time she thought of Ewan's shattered body and mind she felt her lungs constrict, as if the space for them was slowly but surely being minimised. Every time she saw Samantha she felt like a traitor, a fraud, a Judas.

She was responsible for the devastation of Ewan's life.

Eliza twirled the ring on her hand. It was too loose for her now. It had been Samantha's engagement ring, given to her by Ewan's father, Geoff, who had died when Ewan was only five. Samantha had devoted her life to bringing up their son. She had never remarried; she had never even dated anyone else. She had once told Eliza that her few short happy years with Geoff were worth spending the rest of her life alone for. Eliza admired her loyalty and devotion. Few people experienced a love so strong it carried them throughout their entire life.

The traffic was congested getting out of Naples. It seemed as if no one knew the rules, or if they did they were blatantly ignoring them to get where they wanted to go. Tourist buses, taxis, cyclists and people on whining scooters all jostled for position with the occasional death-defying pedestrian thrown into the mix.

Eliza gasped as a scooter cut in on a taxi right in front of them. 'That was ridiculously close!'

Leo gave an indifferent shrug and neatly manoeuvred the car into another lane. 'You get used to it after a while. The tourist season is a little crazy. It's a lot quieter in the off season.'

A long silence ticked past.

'Is your mother still alive?' Eliza asked.

'Yes.'

'Do you ever see her?'

'Not often.'

'So you're not close to her?'

'No.'

There was a wealth of information in that one clipped word, Eliza thought. But then he wasn't the sort of man who got close to anyone. Even when she had met him four years ago he hadn't revealed much about himself. He had told her his parents had divorced when he was a young child and that his mother lived in the US. She hadn't been able to draw him out on the dynamics of his relationship with either parent. He had seemed to her to be a very self-sufficient man who didn't need or want anyone's approval. She had been drawn to that facet of his personality. She had craved acceptance and approval all of her life.

Eliza knew the parent-child relationship was not always rosy. She wasn't exactly the poster girl for happy familial relations. She had made the mistake of tracking down her father a few years ago. Her search had led her to a maximum-security prison. Ron Grady—thank God her mother had never married him—had not been at all interested in her as a daughter, or even as a person. What he had been interested in was turning her into a drug courier. She had walked out and never gone back. 'I'm sorry,' she said. 'It's very painful when you can't relate to a parent.'

'I have no interest in relating to her. She left me when I was barely more than a toddler to run off with her new lover. What sort of mother does that to a little child?'

Troubled mothers, wounded mothers, abused mothers, drug-addicted mothers, under-mothered mothers, Eliza thought sadly. Her own mother had been one of them. She had met them all at one time or the other. She taught their children. She loved their children because they weren't always capable of loving them themselves. 'I don't think it's ever easy being a mother. I think it's harder for some women than others.'

'What about you?' He flicked a quick glance her way. 'Do you plan to have children with your fiancé?'

Eliza looked down at her hands. The diamond of her engagement ring glinted at her in silent conspiracy. 'Ewan is unable to have children.'

The silence hummed for a long moment. She felt it pushing against her ears like two hard hands.

'That must be very hard for someone like you,' he said. 'You obviously love children.'

'I do, but it's not meant to be.'

'What about IVF?'

'It's not an option.'

'Why are you still tied to him if he can't give you what you want?'

'There's such a thing as commitment.' She clenched her hands so hard the diamond of her ring bit into the flesh of her finger. 'I can't just walk away because things aren't going according to plan. Life doesn't always go according to plan. You have to learn to make the best of things—to cope.'

He glanced at her again. 'It seems to me you're not coping as well as you'd like.'

'What makes you say that? You don't know me. We're practically strangers.'

'I know you're not in love.'

Eliza threw him a defensive look. 'Were you in love with your wife?'

A knot of tension pulsed near the corner of his mouth and she couldn't help noticing his hands had tightened slightly on the steering wheel. 'No. But then, she wasn't in love with me, either.'

'Then why did you get married?'

'Giulia got pregnant.'

'That was very noble of you,' Eliza said. 'Not many men show up at the altar because of an unplanned pregnancy these days.'

His knuckles whitened and then darkened as if he was forcing himself to relax his grip on the steering wheel. 'I've always used protection but it failed on the one occasion we slept together. I assumed it was an accident but later she told me she'd done it deliberately. I did the right thing by her and gave her and our daughter my name.'

'It must have made for a tricky relationship.'

He gave her a brief hard glance. 'I love my daughter.

I'm not happy that I was tricked into fatherhood but that doesn't make me love her any less.'

'I wasn't suggesting—'

'I had decided to marry Giulia even if Alessandra wasn't mine.'

'But why?' she asked. 'You said you weren't in love with her.'

'We were both at a crossroads. The man she had expected to marry had jilted her.' His lip curled without humour. 'You could say we had significant common ground.'

Eliza frowned at his little dig at her. 'So it was a pity pick-up for both of you?'

His eyes met hers in a flinty little lock before he returned to concentrating on the traffic. 'Marriage can work just as well, if not better, when love isn't part of the arrangement. And it might have worked for us except Giulia struggled with her mood once Alessandra was born. It was a difficult delivery. She didn't bond with the baby.'

Eliza had met a number of mothers who had struggled with bonding with their babies. The pressure on young mothers to be automatically brilliant at mothering was particularly distressing for those who didn't feel that surge of maternal warmth right at the start. 'I'm very sorry… It must have been very difficult for you, trying to support her through that.'

Lines of bitterness were etched around his mouth. 'Yes. It was.'

He didn't speak much after that. Eliza sat back and looked at the spectacular scenery as they drove along the Amalfi coast towards Positano. But her mind kept going back to his loveless marriage, the reasons for it, the difficulties during it and the tragic way it had ended.

He was left with a small child to rear on his own. Would he look for another wife to help him raise his little girl? Would it be another loveless arrangement or would he seek a more fulfilling relationship this time? She wondered what sort of woman he would settle for. With the sort of wealth he had he could have anyone he wanted. But somehow she couldn't see him settling for looks alone. He would want someone on the same wavelength as him, someone who understood him on a much deeper and meaningful level. He was a complex man who had a lot more going on under the surface than he let on. She had caught a glimpse of that brooding complexity in that bar in Rome four years ago. That dark shuttered gaze, the proud and aloof bearing, and the mantle of loneliness that he took great pains to keep hidden.

Was that why she had connected with him so instantly? They were both lonely souls disappointed by experiences in childhood, doing their best to conceal their innermost pain, reluctant to show any sign of vulnerability in case someone exploited them.

Eliza hadn't realised she had drifted off to sleep until the car came to a stop. She blinked her eyes open and sat up straighter in her seat. The car was in the forecourt of a huge, brightly lit villa that was perched on the edge of a precipitous cliff that overlooked the ocean. 'This isn't the same place you had before,' she said. 'It's much bigger. It must be three times the size.'

Leo opened her door for her. 'I felt like I needed a change.'

She wondered if there had been too many memories of their time together in his old place. They had made love in just about every room and even in the swimming pool. Had he found it impossible to live there once she had left? She had often thought of his quaint little sun-drenched villa tucked into the hillside, how secluded it had been, how they had been mostly left alone, apart from a housekeeper who had come in once a week.

A place this size would need an army of servants to keep it running smoothly. As they walked to the front door Eliza caught a glimpse of a huge swimming pool surrounded by lush gardens out the back. Scarlet bougainvillea clung to the stone wall that created a secluded corner from the sea breeze and the scent of lemon blossom and sun-warmed rosemary was sharp in the air. Tubs of colourful flowers dotted the cobblestone courtyard and a wrought iron trellis of wisteria created a scented canopy that led to a massive marble fountain.

A housekeeper opened the front door even before they got there and greeted them in Italian. 'Signor Valente, *signorina*, *benvenuto*—'

'English please, Marella,' Leo said. 'Miss Lincoln doesn't speak Italian.'

'Actually, I know a little,' Eliza said. 'I had a little boy in my class a couple of years ago who was Italian. I got to know his mother quite well and we gave each other language lessons.'

'I would prefer you to speak English with my daughter,' he said. 'It will help her become more fluent. Marella will show you to your room. I will see you later at dinner.'

Eliza frowned as he strode across the foyer to the grand staircase that swept up in two arms to the floors above. He had dismissed her again as if she was an encumbrance that had been thrust upon him.

'He is under a lot of strain,' Marella said, shaking her head in a despairing manner. 'Working too hard, worrying about the *bambina*; he never stops. His wife…'

She threw her hands in the air. 'Don't get me started about that one. I should not speak ill of the dead, no?'

'It must have been a very difficult time,' Eliza said.

'That child needs a mother,' Marella said. 'But Signor Valente will never marry again, not after the last time.'

'I'm sure if he finds the right person he would be—'

Marella shook her head again. 'What is that saying? Once bitten, twice shy? And who would take on his little girl? Too much trouble for most women.'

'I'm sure Alessandra is a delightful child who just needs some time to adjust to the loss of her mother,' Eliza said. 'It's a huge blow for a young child, but I'm sure with careful handling she'll come through it.'

'Poor little *bambina*.' Marella's eyes watered and she lifted a corner of her apron to wipe at them. 'Come, I will show you to your room. Giuseppe will bring up your bag.'

As Eliza followed the housekeeper upstairs she noticed all the priceless works of art on the walls and in the main gallery on the second level. The amount of wealth it took to have such masters in one's collection was astonishing. And not just paintings—there were marble statues and other objets d'art placed on each landing of the four-storey villa. Plush Persian rugs lay over the polished marble floors and sunlight streamed in long columns from the windows on every landing. It was a rich man's paradise and yet it didn't feel anything like a home.

'Your suite is this one,' Marella said. 'Would you like me to unpack for you?'

'No, thank you, I'll be fine.'

'I'll leave you to settle in,' Marella said. 'Dinner will be at eight-thirty.'

'Where does Alessandra sleep?' Eliza asked.

Marella pointed down the corridor. 'In the nursery; it's the second door from the bathroom on this level. She will be asleep now, otherwise I would take you to her. The agency girl will be on duty until tomorrow so you can relax until then.'

'Wouldn't it be better for me to move into the room closest to the nursery once the agency girl leaves?' Eliza asked.

'Signor Valente told me to put you in this room,' Marella said. 'But I will go and ask him, *sì*?'

'No, don't worry about it right now. I'll talk to him later. I suppose I can't move in while the other girl is there anyway.'

'*Sì, signorina*.'

Eliza stepped inside the beautifully appointed room once the housekeeper had left, the thick rug almost swallowing her feet as she moved across the floor. Crystal chandeliers dangled from the impossibly high ceiling and there were matching sconces on the walls. The suite was painted in a delicate shade of duck egg blue with a gold trim. The furniture was antique; some pieces looked as if they were older than the villa itself. The huge bed with its rich velvet bedhead was made up in snowy white linen with a collection of blue and gold cushions against the pillows in the same shade as the walls. Dark blue velvet curtains were draped either side of the large windows, which overlooked the gardens and the lemon and olive groves in the distance.

Once Eliza had showered and changed she still had half an hour to spare before dinner. She made her way along the wide corridor to the nursery Marella had pointed out. She thought it was probably polite to at least meet the girl from the agency so she could become familiar with Alessandra's routine. But when she got to the door of the nursery it was ajar, although she could hear a shower running in the main bathroom on the other side of the corridor. She considered waiting for the girl to return but curiosity got the better of her. She found herself drawn towards the cot that was against the wall in the nursery.

Eliza looked down at the sleeping child, a dark-haired angel with alabaster skin, her tiny starfish hands splayed either side of her head as she slept. Sooty-black eyelashes fanned her little cheeks, her rosebud mouth slightly open as her breath came in and then out. She looked small for her age, petite, almost fragile. Eliza reached over the side of the cot and gently brushed a dark curl back off the tiny forehead, a tight fist of maternal longing clutching at her insides.

This could have been our child.

The thought of never having a child of her own was something that grieved and haunted her. All of her life she had craved a family of her own. Becoming engaged to Ewan when she was only nineteen had been part of her plan to create a solid family base. She hadn't wanted to wait until she was older. She had planned to get married and have children while she was young, to build the secure base she had missed out on.

But life had a habit of messing with one's carefully laid out plans.

There was a part cry, part murmur from the cot. '*Mamma?*'

Eliza felt a hand grasp at her heart at that plaintive sound. 'It's all right, Alessandra,' she said as she stroked the little girl's silky head again. 'Shh, now, go back to sleep.'

The child's little hand found hers and she curled her

fingers around two of hers although she didn't appear to be fully awake. Her eyes were still closed, those thick lashes resting against her pale cheeks like miniature fans. After a while her breathing evened out and her little body relaxed on a sigh that tugged again at Eliza's heartstrings.

She looked at the tiny fingers that were clinging to hers. How tragic that one so young had lost her mother. Who would she turn to as she grew through her childhood into her teens and then as a young woman—nannies and carers and a host of lovers that came and went in Leo's life? What sort of upbringing would that be? Eliza knew what it was like to be handed back and forth like a parcel nobody wanted. All her life she had tried to heal the wound the death of her mother had left. Of feeling that it was *her* fault her mother had died. Would it be the same for little Alessandra? Feeling guilty that she was somehow the cause of her mother giving up on life? Of constantly seeking to fill the aching void in her soul?

There was a sound from the door and Eliza turned and saw Leo standing there watching her with an unreadable expression on his face. 'Where's Laura, the agency girl?' he asked.

'I think she's having a shower. I was just going past and I—'

'You're not on duty until the morning.'

Eliza didn't care for being reprimanded for doing something that came as naturally to her as breathing. Sleeping children needed checking on. Distressed children needed comforting. She raised her chin at him. 'Your daughter seemed restless. She called out to her mother. I comforted her back to sleep.'

Something moved through his eyes, a rapid flash of

pain that was painful to witness. 'Marella is waiting to dish up dinner.' He held open the door for her in a pointed fashion. 'I'll see you downstairs.'

'She looks like you.' The words were out before Eliza could stop them.

It was a moment or two before he spoke. 'Yes…' His expression remained inscrutable but she sensed an inner tension that he seemed at great pains to keep hidden.

She swallowed against the tide of regret that rose in her throat. If things had been different they would both be leaning over that cot as the proud, devoted parents of that gorgeous little girl. They might have even had another baby on the way by now. The family she had longed for, the family she had dreamed about for most of her life could have been hers but for that one fateful night that had changed the entire course of her life.

'*Mamma*?'

Eliza swung her gaze to the cot where Alessandra had now pulled herself upright, her little dimpled hands clinging to the rail. She rubbed at one of her eyes with a little fisted hand. 'I want *Mamma*,' she whimpered as her chin started to wobble.

Eliza went over to the cot and picked up the little toddler and cuddled her close. 'I'm not your mummy but I've come to take care of you for a little while,' she said as she stroked the child's back in a soothing and rhythmic manner.

Alessandra tried to wriggle away. 'I want Kathleen.'

'Kathleen had to go and see her family,' Eliza said, rocking her gently from side to side. 'She'll be back before you know it.'

'Where's *Papà*?' Alessandra asked.

'I'm here, *mia piccolo*.' Leo's voice was gentle as he placed his hand on his daughter's raven-black head.

The base of Eliza's spine quivered at his closeness. She could smell his citrus-based aftershave; she could even smell the fabric softener that clung to the fibres of his shirt. Her senses were instantly on high alert. Her left shoulder was within touching distance of his chest. She could feel the solid wall of him just behind her. She was so tempted to lean against the shelter of his body. It had been so long since she had felt someone put their arms around her and hold her close.

'I wetted the bed,' Alessandra said sheepishly.

Eliza could feel the dampness against her arm where the little tot's bottom was resting. She glanced up at Leo, who gave her a don't-blame-me look. 'She refuses to wear a nappy to bed,' he said.

'I'm too big for nappies,' Alessandra announced with a cute little pout of her rosebud mouth, although her deep-set eyes were still half closed. 'I'm a big girl now.'

'I'm sure you are,' Eliza said. 'But even big girls need a bit of help now and again, especially at night. Maybe you could wear pull-ups for a while. They're much more grown-up. I've seen some really cool ones with little pink kittens on them. I can get some for you if you like.'

Alessandra plugged a thumb in her mouth by way of answer. It seemed this was one little Munchkin who was rather practised in getting her own way.

'Let's get you changed, shall we?' Eliza said as she carried the little girl to the changing table in the corner of the nursery. 'Do you want the pink pyjamas or the blue ones?'

'I don't know my colours,' Alessandra said from around her thumb.

'Well, maybe I can teach you while I'm here,' Eliza said.

'You'd be wasting your time,' Leo said.

Eliza glanced at him with a reproving frown. Little children should not be exposed to negative messages about their capacity to learn. It could set up a lifelong pattern of failure. ‘Pardon?’ she said.

‘My daughter will never learn her colours.’

‘That’s ridiculous,’ she said. ‘Why ever not?’

He gave her a grim look. ‘Because she is blind.’

CHAPTER FOUR

ELIZA BLINKED AT him in shock.

Blind?

Her heart clanged against her ribcage like a pendulum struck by a sledgehammer.

Alessandra was blind?

Her emotions went into a downward spiral. How cruel! How impossibly cruel that this little child was not only motherless but blind as well. It was so tragic, so unbearable to think that Leo's little girl couldn't see the world around her, not even the faces of the people she loved.

How devastating for him as a father. How gut-wrenching to think of all the obstacles that little mite would face over her lifetime. All the things she would miss out on or not be able to enjoy as others enjoyed them. The beauty of the world she would never see. It was so sad, so tragic it made Eliza's heart ache for Leo. It made her ache for the little toddler who lived in a world of blackness. 'I'm sorry…I didn't realise…'

'Will you tell me a story?' Alessandra piped up from the changing table.

'Of course,' Eliza said. 'But after that you have to go back to sleep.' Oh, dear God, how did the little babe even know it was night? Anguish squeezed the breath out of her chest. She felt as if she was being suffocated by it. How had Leo coped with such a tragic blow? Was that why his wife had ended her life? Had it been too much for her to cope with a child who was blind?

The agency girl, Laura, came in at that point. 'Oh, sorry,' she said. 'Is she awake? I thought she'd settled for the night.'

'My daughter's bed needs changing,' Leo said curtly.

'I'll see to it,' Laura said and rushed over to the cot.

Eliza had finished the business end of things with Alessandra and gathered her up in her arms again. 'I have just the story for you,' she said and carried her back to the freshly made up cot. 'Do you like dogs?'

'Yes, but Papà won't let me have a puppy,' Alessandra said in a baleful tone. 'He said I have to wait until I'm older. I don't want to wait until I'm older. I want one now.'

'I'm sure he knows what's best for you,' Eliza said. 'Now, let's get you settled in bed before I start my story.'

'Where's Kathleen?' Alessandra asked. 'Why isn't she here? I want Kathleen. I want her now!' Those little heels began to drum against the mattress of the cot.

'I told you she had a family emergency to see to,' Leo said.

'But I want her here with me!' Alessandra said, starting to wail again.

Eliza could see that Alessandra was a very bright child who was used to pushing against the boundaries. It was common after the death of a parent for the remaining parent or other carers to overcompensate for their loss. It was just as common for a child with a disability to be treated the same way. The little girl was used to being the centre of attention and used every opportunity she could to grasp at power.

'Kathleen is going to be away for the next month,' she said. 'But I think it might be nice if Papà gets her to call you on the phone while she's away.'

'Does she miss me?'

'I'm sure she does,' Eliza said. 'Now, let's get those feet of yours still and relaxed, otherwise my story won't come out to play.'

'How long are you staying?' Alessandra asked.

Eliza glanced at Leo but his expression was as blank as a mask. 'Let's not worry about that just now,' she said. 'The important thing is that you get back to sleep. Now, let's see how this goes. Once upon a time there was a little dog who loved to chase…'

'Asleep?' Leo asked as Eliza joined him downstairs a few minutes later.

'Yes.' She came over to where he was standing and looked up at him with a frown. 'Why on earth didn't you tell me?'

'I did tell you.'

'I meant right from the start.'

'Touché and all that.' He gave an indifferent shrug of one broad shoulder before he took a sip from the drink he was holding.

Eliza gave him a cross look. 'You should've told me at the beginning.'

'Would it have influenced your decision in taking up the post?'

'No, but I would've liked to know what I'm dealing with. I could've prepared myself better.' *I could have got all this confusing emotion out of the way so I could think straight.*

'Yes, well, life doesn't always give one the chance to prepare for what it has in store.'

Tell me about it, Eliza thought. 'She's a lovely child but clearly a little headstrong.'

His look was brittle. 'Are you saying I'm a bad parent?'

'Of course not,' she said. 'It's very clear you love her as any good parent should. It's just that it seems she's in control of everyone who has anything to do with her. That's very stressful for young children. She needs to know who is in charge. It's especially important for a child with special needs. How long has she—?'

'She's been blind from birth.'

Eliza felt her heart tighten all over again. It was a cramped ache deep in her chest. 'That must have been a huge blow to you and your wife.' How she hated having to say those words—*your wife.*

'It was. Giulia never quite got her head around it. She blamed herself.'

'It seems to me every mother blames herself no matter what the circumstances.'

'Perhaps, but in Giulia's case it was particularly difficult. She thought she was being punished for setting me up.'

'Did *you* blame her?' Eliza asked.

His brows came together over his dark eyes. 'Of course not. It was no one's fault. Alessandra was premature. She has retrolental hyperplasia. It was previously thought to be caused by an excess of oxygen in perinatal care but there's divided opinion between specialists on that now. It's also called ROP. Retinopathy of Prematurity.'

'Can nothing be done?' Eliza asked. 'There are advances happening in medicine all the time. Surely there's something that can be done for her?'

'There is nothing anyone can do. Alessandra can

only distinguish light from dark. She is legally and permanently blind.'

Eliza could hear the pain in his voice but it was even more notable in his expression. No wonder those grey hairs had formed at his temples, and no wonder his eyes and mouth were etched with those lines. What parent could receive such news about their child without it tearing them apart both physically and emotionally?

'I'm so very sorry. I can't imagine how tough this has been for you and will no doubt continue to be.'

'I want the best for my daughter.' His expression was taut with determination. 'There is nothing I won't do to make sure she has a happy and fulfilled life.'

Eliza wasn't quite sure what role she was meant to play in order to give Alessandra the best possible chance in life. The child had suffered enough disruption already without a fly-in, fly-out nanny to confuse her further. What Alessandra needed was a predictable and secure routine. She needed stability and a nurturing environment.

She needed her mother.

The aching sadness of it struck Eliza anew. How devastating for a little toddler to have lost the most important person in her life. How terrifying it must be for little Alessandra when she woke during the night and wanted the comfort of her mother's arms, only to find a series of paid nannies to see to her needs. No wonder she was difficult. Even a sighted child would be hard to manage after suffering the loss of her mother.

'What do you hope to gain for her from my period as her nanny?' she asked.

'You're an excellent teacher. You understand small children.'

'I've never worked with a vision impaired child before, only a profoundly deaf one,' Eliza said.

'I'm sure you'll find a way to make the most of your time with her,' he said. 'After all, I'm paying you top dollar.'

She frowned. 'It's not about the money.'

A dark brow arched over his left eye. 'No?'

'Of course not.' She pulled at her lip momentarily with her teeth. 'Don't get me wrong—I'm happy about your donation to the school, but I'm not in this for what I can get for myself. I'm not that sort of person.'

'Is your fiancé rich?'

Eliza felt the searing penetration of his cynical gaze. The insurance payout from the accident, along with the modest trust fund his late father had bequeathed Ewan had provided a reasonably secure income for the rest of his life. Without it, he and his mother, who was his chief carer, would have really struggled. 'He has enough to provide for his…I mean our future.'

'What does he do for a living?' Leo asked.

She looked at him numbly. What could she say? Should she tell him about Ewan's accident? Would it make a difference to how he thought of her? Explaining the accident would mean revealing her part in it. She could still see Ewan's face, the shock in his eyes and the pain of rejection in every plane and contour of his face. He had looked as if she had dealt him a physical blow. Even his colour had faded to a chalk-white pallor. For so long since she had wondered if she could have prepared him better for her decision to end things. It must have come as such a dreadful shock to him for her to announce it so seemingly out of the blue. She had been struggling with their relationship for months but hadn't said anything. But over that time she had found it harder and harder to envisage a future with him. Her love for him had been more like one would have for a friend rather than a life partner. Sex had become a bit of a chore for her. But she had felt so torn because he and his mother were the only family she had known after a lifetime of foster home placements.

And he had loved her.

That had always been the hardest thing to get her head around when it came to her final decision to end things. Ewan had loved her from the first moment he had helped her pick up the books she had dropped on her first day of term in sixth form after she had been placed with yet another foster family. She'd been the new kid in town and he had taken her under his wing and helped her to fit in. Being loved by someone had been a new experience for her. Up until that point she had always felt out of place, a burden that people put up with because it was the right thing to do for a kid in need. Being loved by Ewan had made her feel better about herself, more worthy, beautiful even.

But she hadn't loved him the same way he loved her.

'He has his own business,' she finally said, which was in a way not quite a lie. 'Investments, shares, that sort of thing.'

Marella came in just then, which shifted the conversation in another direction once they had taken their places at the table.

Eliza didn't feel much like eating. Her stomach was knotted and her temples were throbbing, signalling a tension headache was well on its way. She looked across at Leo and he didn't seem to be too hungry either. He had barely touched his entrée and took only a token couple of sips of the delicious wine he had poured for them both. His brow was furrowed and his posture tense. She sensed a brooding anger in him that he was trying to control for the sake of politeness or maybe because he was concerned Marella would come in on them with the rest of their meal.

'You blame me, don't you?' Eliza said into the cavernous silence.

His eyes were like diamonds, hard and impenetrable. 'What makes you say that?'

She drew in a sharp breath as she put her napkin aside. 'Look—I understand your frustration and despair over your daughter's condition but I hardly see that I'm in any way to blame.'

He pushed back from his chair so quickly the glasses on the table rattled. 'You lied to me,' he said through tight lips. 'You lied to me from the moment we met.'

Eliza rose to her feet rather than have him tower over her so menacingly. 'You lied to yourself, Leo. You wanted a wife and you chose the first woman to fit your checklist.'

'Why did you come on to me in that bar that night?

She found it hard to hold his burning gaze. 'I was at a loose end. I was jet-lagged and lonely. I have no other excuse. I would never do something like that normally. I can't really explain it even now.'

'Let me tell you why you did it.' His top lip curled in disdain. 'You were feeling horny. Your fiancé was thousands of miles away. You needed a stand-in stud to scratch your itch.'

'Stop it!' Eliza clamped her hands over her ears. 'Stop saying such horrible things.'

He pulled her hands down from her face, his fingers like handcuffs around her wrists. The blood sizzled in her veins at the contact. She felt every pore of her skin flare to take more of him in. Her inner core contracted as her body remembered how it had felt to have him thrusting inside her. His first possession four years ago had been rough, almost animalistic and yet she had relished every heart-stopping, pulse-racing second of it.

'You still want it, don't you?'

'No,' she said but her body was already betraying her. It moved towards him, searching for him, hungering for him, *aching* for him.

'Liar.' He brought her chin up, his eyes blazing with fiery intent.

'Don't do this,' she said but she wasn't sure if she was pleading with him or herself.

'You still want me. I saw it that first day when I came to your flat.'

'You're wrong.' She tried to deny it even as her pelvis brushed against his in feverish need.

He grasped her by the bottom and pushed her hard into his arousal. 'That's what you want, isn't it? You're desperate for it, just like you were four years ago.'

Eliza tried to push him away but it was like a stick insect trying to shift a skyscraper from its foundations. 'Stop it,' she begged. 'Please stop saying that.' A bubble of emotion rose in her throat. She tried to swallow it back down but it refused to go away. She didn't want to break down in front of him. She hated that weakness in her, the one where she became overwhelmed and crumbled emotionally. It was the abandoned little seven-year-old girl in her who did that.

She wasn't that little girl any more.

She was strong and independent.

She *had* to be strong.

She had to survive.

She had to withstand the temptation of losing herself in the sensual world of Leo Valente, the one man who could dismantle her carefully constructed emotional armour. Her armour had been just fine until he had come along. It had always stood her in good stead. But now it was peeling off her like a sloughed skin, leaving her exposed and raw and vulnerable.

'I'm sorry…' She squeezed her eyes tightly closed for a moment. 'I just need a little minute…'

He dropped his hold as if she had suddenly burned him. 'Save your tears.' He scraped a hand through his hair. 'It's not your pity I'm after.'

Eliza forced her eyes back to his hardened cynical gaze. 'Right now I'm having a little trouble figuring out what it is you actually want from me.'

'I told you. I want you to fill in for Kathleen. That's all I want.'

She watched as he strode to the other side of the room, his movements like his words: clipped and tense. Was it true? Was that *all* he wanted from her? What if he wanted more? Wasn't it too late? An unbridgeable chasm separated them. He'd had a child with another woman. She was still tied to another man. Even if they wanted to be together, how could she desert Ewan when it was her fault he was sitting drooling in that chair?

Maybe this *was* about revenge. It pained her to think Leo would stoop to that. Was he so bitter that he had to make her suffer? What good would it do to either of them to spend a month at war over what had happened four years ago? It wouldn't change anything. Their history would still be the same. Their future would still be hopelessly unattainable.

'You should go to bed.' Leo turned to look at her again. 'Alessandra is not an easy child to manage. You'll need all your reserves to handle her.'

'I'm used to dealing with difficult children,' Eliza said. 'I've made a career out of it.'

'Indeed you have.' He gave her a brief on-off movement of his lips that was a paltry imitation of a smile. 'Goodnight, Eliza.'

She felt as if she was being dismissed again. It didn't sit comfortably with her. She wanted to spend more time with him, getting to know the man he was now. Understanding the agony he was going through in handling a blind, motherless child. He seemed lonely and isolated. She could see it now that she knew what had put that guarded look in his eyes and that tension in the way he held his body. Who was helping him deal with his little girl's disability? Was anyone supporting him? She had met parents of special needs kids before. They carried a huge weight of responsibility on their shoulders. They had told her how shocking and devastating it had been to find they were now members of a club they had never intended to join: the autism club, the hearing impaired club, the learning disabled club—the not quite perfect club. And in most cases it wasn't a temporary membership.

It was for life.

'Leo…' She took a step towards him but then stopped when she saw the dark glitter of his gaze. 'I think it's important for Alessandra if she senses that we are friends rather than enemies.'

'How do you propose we do that?'

Eliza felt the mesmerising pull of his gaze. He was so close she could see the dark pepper of his stubble and her fingers twitched to reach up and feel its sexy rasp against her fingertips. She looked at his mouth, her stomach clenching as she remembered how passionately those lips could kiss and conquer hers. Her insides coiled as she thought of how he had explored every inch of her body with his lips and tongue. Was he remembering it too? Was he replaying every erotic scene in his head and feeling the reaction reverberate through his body? 'I…I think it's important we be civil to each other…'

'Civil?' Those fathomless dark eyes burned and seared as they held hers.

'Yes…civil…polite…that sort of thing.' She swallowed a tight little restriction in her throat. 'There's no need for us to be trading insults. We're both mature adults and I think it's best if we try and act as if we… um, like each other…a bit…at least while we're in the presence of Alessandra.'

'And what about when we are alone?' One of his brows lifted in a sardonic arc. 'Are we to continue to pretend to like each other—*a bit*?'

Something about his tone sent a shiver to the base of Eliza's spine. Being alone with him was something she was going to have to avoid as much as possible. The temptation of being in his arms had always been her downfall. Hadn't his rough embrace just proved it? He had only to touch her and her body burst into hungry flames of need. He said he didn't want her, but she saw the glitter of lust in his eyes. He could deny it all he liked but she could feel it like a third presence in the room. It hovered there between them, a silent but ever-present reminder of every erotic interlude they had shared.

His body *knew* hers intimately.

He knew how responsive she was to his touch. He knew how to make her flesh hum and sing. His touch on her body was like a delicate, priceless instrument being played by a maestro. No one could make her body respond the way he did. He was doing it now just by looking at her with that dark assessing gaze. It stroked her as it moved over her body. She felt the fizz and tingle of her lips as his gaze lingered there as if he was recalling how they had felt against his own. She felt a prickly stirring in her breasts when his gaze moved over them. Was he remembering how her tight nipples had felt against his teeth and tongue? Was he remembering how she had whimpered in pleasure as his teeth had sexily grazed her sensitive flesh? She felt the heat of arousal between her thighs even without him lowering his gaze that far. Was he remembering how it had felt to plunge his body into hers until they had both careened into mindless oblivion?

'I'm not here to spend time alone with you.' She gave him an arch look. 'I'm here to look after your daughter. That's what I'm being paid to do, isn't it?'

His gaze was inscrutable but she could see a tiny muscle clenching on and off in his jaw. 'Indeed it is.' He moved to the door. 'I'm going out for a short while. I don't know what time I'll be back.'

'Where are you going?' She mentally grimaced. She hadn't meant to sound like a waspish wife checking up on him.

He gave her a satirical look. 'Where do you think I might be going?'

Eliza felt her stomach plummet in despair. *He had a mistress.* No wonder he had pulled away from her. He already had someone else who saw to those needs. Who was she? Was it someone local? Had he set her up in a villa close by? Please don't let it be their villa—the villa where she had spent those blissful three weeks with him.

She set her mouth in a contemptuous line. 'Nice to

see you haven't let the minor inconvenience of widowhood and single parenthood get in the way of your sex life.'

His dark eyes glinted warningly. 'You are not being paid to comment on any aspect of my private life.'

'Did you get her to sign a confidentiality agreement too?' She threw him an icy glare. 'Did you pay her heaps and heaps of money to keep her mouth shut and her legs open?'

The silence was so tense it rang like the high-pitched whistle of a cheap kettle.

Eliza felt his anger. It was billowing in the air between them like invisible smoke. It sucked all the oxygen out of the room until she found it hard to breathe. She had overstepped the mark. She had let her emotions gallop out of control. She had revealed her vulnerability to him.

'Isn't jealousy a little inconsistent of you, given you're wearing another man's ring?' he asked in a deceptively calm tone.

She forced herself to hold his gaze. 'Relationships are not meant to be business contracts. You can't do that to people. It's not right.'

His lip curled mockingly. 'Let me get this straight—*you're* telling me what's right and wrong?'

She drew in a sharp breath to try to harness her spiralling emotions. 'I'm sorry. I shouldn't have said anything. It's none of my business who you see or what arrangements you make in order to see them.'

'You're damn right it's none of your business.'

Eliza bit down on her lip as he strode out of the room, flinching when he clipped the door shut behind him. The sound of his car roaring to life outside was like a glancing blow to her heart. She listened to him drive out of the villa grounds, her imagination already torturing her with where he was going and what he would be doing when he got there.

CHAPTER FIVE

LEO UNMOORED HIS motor launch and motored out to a favourite spot where he could look back at the twinkling lights fringing the Amalfi coast. He dropped anchor and sat on the deck, listening to the gentle slap of the water against the hull and the musical clanging of the rigging against the mast of a distant yacht as the onshore breeze passed through. A gibbous moon cast a silver glow across the crinkled surface of the ocean. It was the closest he got to peace these days, out here on the water.

It was laughably ironic that Eliza thought he was off bedding a mistress. He hadn't been with anyone since Giulia had died ten months ago. Not that his relationship with her had been fulfilling in that department. He had tried to make it work a couple of times in the early days, but he had always known she was lying there wishing he were someone else.

Hadn't he done the same?

He hadn't wanted to hurt her by treating her as a substitute, so in the end they had agreed on a sexless arrangement. He could have had affairs; Giulia had told him to do whatever he had to do and she would turn a blind eye, but he hadn't pursued it. He had the normal urges of any other man his age, but he had ignored them to focus on his responsibilities as a parent and his ever-demanding career.

But his physical reaction to Eliza was a pretty potent reminder that he couldn't go on ignoring the needs of his body. He had wanted her so badly it had taken every ounce of self-control not to back her up against the nearest wall and do what they both did so well together. His groin was still tingling with the sensation of her body jammed tightly against his. He had felt the soft press of her beautiful breasts against his chest. He had desperately wanted to cover her mouth with his, to rediscover those sensual contours, to taste the hot sweetness of her.

He had intended to keep his distance during her short stay. He had been so confident he would be able to keep things on a business level between them. But, reflecting on it now, he could see how that call from Kathleen when he was in London for his meeting had completely thrown him. He was used to having his life carefully controlled. His domestic arrangements ran like clockwork. He had come to rely heavily on his staff, almost forgetting they had lives and families and issues of their own. When Kathleen had begged him for some time off he'd had to think on his feet and the first person he had thought of was Eliza. He'd told himself it was because she was a talented teacher and used to handling difficult and needy children. But what if the subconscious part of him had made the decision for a completely different reason?

He still wanted her.

Who was he kidding? Of course he still wanted her. But would a month be enough to end this torment that plagued him? Those three weeks he'd had with her had never left his memory. He could recall almost every passionate moment they had spent together. The memory of her body lived in his flesh. When he looked at her he felt his blood stir. He felt his heart rate rise. He felt his skin tingle in anticipation of her silky touch. The need to possess her was a persistent ache. Seeing her again had brought it all back. The blistering passion she evoked in him. The heat and fire of her response that made him feel as if she was his perfect mate—that there was no one else out there who could make him feel the way she did. It was going to be impossible to ignore the desire he had for her when every time he came within touching distance of her his body reacted so powerfully.

But wouldn't an affair with her create more problems, which he could do without right now?

On the other hand, he was used to compartmentalising his life. He could file his relationship with her into the temporary basket. Wasn't that what she would want? It wasn't as if she was going to end her engagement for him. She'd had four years to do so and yet she hadn't.

He didn't understand how she could sell herself so short. What was she getting out of her relationship with her fiancé that she couldn't get with *him*? He had offered her riches beyond measure, a lifetime of love and commitment, and yet she had thrown it back in his face. Why? What tied her to a man who *still* hadn't married her? He didn't even *live* with her. What hold did he have over her? Or was Eliza keeping a 'fiancé' up her sleeve so she could flit in and out of any shallow little hook-up that took her fancy? The ring she wore didn't look like a modern design. What if she just wore it for show? What if it was her get-out prop? '*Sorry, but I'm already taken*' was a very good way of getting out of a relationship that had run its course. She might have picked the ring up at a pawn shop for all he knew. If there was an actual fiancé Leo was almost certain she wasn't in love with him. How could she be when she looked at him with such raw longing? He was sure he wasn't imagining it. From the first moment he had laid eyes on her he had felt an electric connection that was beyond anything he had felt before or since.

But this time he wouldn't be offering her anything but an affair. He gave a twisted smile. A shallow hook-up was what he would offer. He would set the rules. He would set the boundaries and he would enforce them if he had to. He would not think about the morality of it. If she was willing to betray her fiancé—if there was one—then it was nothing to do with him.

She could always say no.

By two a.m. Eliza had given up on the notion of sleeping. It wasn't the jetlag or the strange bed. It was the restlessness of her body that was keeping her from slumber. A milky drink usually did the trick but could she risk running into Leo by going downstairs to get one? She hadn't heard him return, but then, why would he need to? He had plenty of staff to keep his household running while he indulged in an off-site affair with his latest mistress.

Eliza slipped on a wrap and went downstairs. There was enough moonlight coming in through the windows to light her way. Just as she was taking the last step down, the front door opened. She gave a little startled gasp and put her hand up to the throat where her heart seemed to have jumped. 'Leo?'

He gave her a wry look. 'Who else were you expecting?'

Eliza pursed her lips. 'I wasn't expecting anyone. And I wasn't waiting up for you, either.'

A mocking glint shone in his dark eyes. 'Of course not.'

She jutted her chin at him. 'I was on my way to the kitchen to get a hot drink.'

'Don't let me stop you.'

Eliza looked at his tousled hair. *Bed hair. Just had wild sex hair.* It maddened her to think he could just waltz in and parade his sexual conquests like a badge of honour. 'How was your evening? Did it live up to your expectations?'

Even in the muted light she could see the way his mouth was slanted with a cat-that-got-the-canary smile. 'It was very pleasurable.'

Jealousy was like an arrow to her belly. How could he stand there and be so…so *blatant* about it?

'I just bet it was.'

'You would know.'

Her brows shot together. 'What's that supposed to mean?'

His smile had tilted even further to give him a devilish look. 'You've had first-hand experience at spending many a pleasurable evening with me, have you not?'

Eliza tightened her mouth. She didn't want to be reminded of the nights she had spent rolling and screaming with pleasure in his bed. She had spent the last four years *trying* to forget. She threw him a dismissive look. 'Sorry to burst the bubble on your ego, but you haven't left that much of an impression on me. I can barely recall anything about our affair other than I was relieved when it was over.'

'You're lying.'

Eliza gave him a flinty glare. 'That's what really irks you, isn't it, Leo? It still rankles even after all this time. I was the first woman to ever say no to you. You could have anyone you wanted but you couldn't have me.'

'I could have you.' His eyes burned with primal intent. 'I could have you right now and we both know it.'

She gave a scornful laugh that belied the shockingly shaky ground she was desperately trying to stand on. 'I'd like to see you try.'

His eyes scorched hers as he closed the distance between them in a lazy stroll that sent an anticipatory shiver dancing down the length of her spine. She knew *that* look. It made her blood race through the circuitry of her veins like high-octane fuel. It made her heart thud with excitement and her legs tremble like a tripod on an uneven floor. It made her core clench with an ache that had no cure other than the driving force of his body.

He took her by the upper arms, his fingers digging into her flesh with almost brutal strength. 'You should know me well enough by now to know how foolish it is to throw a gauntlet down like that before me.'

Eliza suppressed another little shiver as she flashed him a defiant look. 'I'm not scared of you.'

His fingers tightened even further as he jerked her hard against him. 'Then perhaps you should be.' And then his mouth swooped down and slammed against hers.

It was a bruising kiss but Eliza was beyond caring. The crush of his mouth on hers brought all of her suppressed longings to the surface of her body like lava out of a volcano. She felt the raw need on her lips where his were pressed so forcefully. She felt it in her breasts as they were pushed up against his chest. She felt it unfurling deep in her core, that twisting, twirling, torturous ache that was moving throughout her body at breakneck speed.

How had she gone for so long without feeling this feverish rush of passion? It was like waking up after a decade of sleep. Every pore of her skin was alive and sensitised. Every muscle and sinew was crying out for the stroke and glide of his touch.

His tongue stroked hers until she was whimpering at the back of her throat. His hands were still hard on her upper arms, his fingertips gripping her with bruising force, but she relished in the feel of his commanding hold. His proudly aroused body was pressed intimately against her. She felt the hard ridge of him against the femininity of her body. The barrier of their clothes was torture. She wanted him naked and inside her, filling her, stretching her—making her feel alive in a way no one else could. She moved against him, speaking in a silent and primal feminine language that was universal.

But, instead of answering the call to mate, he dropped his hold and pulled back from her. He wiped the back of his hand across his mouth as if to remove the taste of her. It was a deliberately insulting gesture and she wanted to slap him for it. But she would rather die than show him how much he had hurt her.

'You've certainly got the Neanderthal routine down pat,' she said, pushing back her hair with a flick of her hand. 'I'm surprised you didn't haul me upstairs by the hair to your lair.'

His dark eyes mocked her. 'Surprised or disappointed?'

She held his look with a sassy one of her own. 'I wouldn't have done it, you know. I wouldn't have slept with you.'

The corner of his mouth kicked up cynically. 'No?'

'I was playing with you.' She straightened her wrap over her shoulders with fastidious attention to detail. 'Seeing how far you'd go.'

When she finally brought her gaze back to his another involuntary shiver trickled down her spine at the sexy, *knowing* glint shining there.

'You know where to find me if you feel like playing some more. My room is three doors down from yours. You don't have to knock. Just come right in. I'll be waiting for you.'

Eliza gave him a crushing look. 'Your confidence is seriously misplaced.'

His mouth tilted sardonically as he turned to make his way up the stairs. 'So is yours.'

Eliza was up early the following morning. Not that she had slept much during the night. The needs Leo had awakened made her feel restless and twitchy. All night long her mind had raced with a flood of memories of their past affair—racy little scenes where she had pleasured him or he had pleasured her. Erotic little flashbacks of her lying pinned beneath his rocking body, or her riding him on top until she gasped out loud. They all came back to haunt her—to torture her with the gnawing ache of want that refused to be suppressed. Was that why he had stepped back when he did? He wanted to make her *own* her need of him. He was playing with her like a cat did with a hapless mouse.

She wasn't going to let him break her. She knew he wanted her pride as a trophy. He wanted to have all the power, to be able to control what happened between them this time around. She understood his motivations. She had hurt him. She *regretted* that.

But on the battleground between them was a small defenceless child.

It wasn't fair to let Alessandra get hurt by the crossfire. Any arguments they had would have to be conducted in private. Any resentment would have to be shelved until they were alone.

As she was dressing after her shower Eliza noticed her upper arms bore the faint but unmistakable imprint of his fingers where he had gripped her the night before. It made her belly quiver to think he had branded her with his touch. She slipped on a three quarter length cardigan to cover the marks. She didn't want to have to explain to Marella or to Laura, the agency girl, how they had got there.

Laura was all packed up ready to leave when Eliza went to the nursery suite. 'Alessandra's still asleep,' she said, nodding towards the little girl's room. 'That's the best she's slept since I've been here. She's been a little terror the whole time. I don't think she's slept two hours straight before. You must have a magic touch.'

'I don't know about that,' Eliza said with a self-deprecating smile.

Laura lugged her backpack over one shoulder. 'I'd better get going. I have a ride waiting for me downstairs.' She offered her hand. 'Good luck with it all. I don't envy you having to answer to Leo Valente. He's quite intimidating, isn't he?'

'He's just being a protective father.'

Laura grunted. 'Yeah, well, I wouldn't want to get on the wrong side of him. Did you know him before or something? I don't mean to pry, it's just that last night I kind of got the impression you two knew each other.'

'I met him briefly a few years ago.' Eliza knew she had to be careful what she said. The confidentiality agreement Leo had made her sign made her think twice before she revealed anything about her previous connection with him. She couldn't risk being quoted out of context. She had no reason to believe he wouldn't be true to his word over the consequences of speaking out of turn. There was a streak of ruthlessness in him now that hadn't been there before. Didn't last night prove it?

'You dated him?' Laura probed.

'Not for long. It wasn't serious.'

Laura gave her a streetwise smile. 'Maybe you could have another crack at it. He's got loads and loads of money. He'd be quite a catch if you could put up with the foul temper.'

'I'm already engaged.'

Laura glanced at her left hand. 'Oh, I didn't realise. Sorry. When's the big day?'

'Yes, when is the big day?' Leo's deep voice spoke from behind them.

Eliza felt her face flood with colour as his gaze hit hers. She wondered how long he had been there. Long enough if that brooding look was anything to go by. 'Laura is just leaving, aren't you, Laura?'

'Yes,' Laura said and made a move for the door. 'I'll see myself out. Bye.'

A prickly silence filled the room once the young woman had left.

'I'd prefer you to refrain from gossiping with the hired help,' Leo said in a clipped tone. 'It's in your contract.'

'I wasn't gossiping. I was simply answering her questions. It would've been rude not to.'

'You're not here to answer questions. You're here to look after my daughter.'

Eliza returned his hardened glare. 'Is that *really* why I'm here? Or it is because you have an axe to grind? Revenge is a dirty word, Leo. It's a dirty deed that could turn out hurting you much more than it hurts me.'

His cleanly shaven jaw locked with tension. 'I'd have

to care about you for you to be able to hurt me. I care nothing for you. I only want your body and you want mine. Last night proved it.'

Anger pulsed in her veins at his arrogant dismissal of her as a person. 'Do you really think I would allow myself to be used like that? To be pawed over like some cheap two-bit hooker you hired off a dark alley?'

There was a condescending glitter in his eyes as they warred with hers. 'I'd hardly call a million pounds cheap. But you can forget about bargaining for more. I'm not paying it. You're not worth it.'

'Oh, I'm worth it, all right.' She put on her best sultry come-to-bed-with-me look. 'I'm worth every penny and more.'

He grasped her so suddenly the breath was knocked right out of her lungs. She felt the imprint of his fingers on the bruises he had left the day before but her pride would not allow her to wince or flinch. 'You want me just as much as I want you. I know the game you're playing. You want to drive up the price. I've sorted out your school, but it's *your* bank account you want sorted out now, isn't it?'

Eliza couldn't stop herself from looking at his mouth. It was flat-lined and bitter now, but she remembered all too well how soft and sensual it could be when it came into contact with hers. Desire flooded her being. She felt the on-off contraction of it deep in her core. He was the only man who could reduce her to this—to this primal need that would settle for nothing less than the explosive possession of his body. Could she withstand this temptation? Could she work for him without giving in to this desperate longing?

'I don't need your money.'

He gave one of his harsh laughs. 'But you'd like it all the same. You're starting to realise what you've thrown away, aren't you?'

'I always knew what I was throwing away.'

His top lip curled. 'Are you saying you have regrets?'

She arched her brow pointedly. 'Don't we all?'

He held her gaze in a stare-down that made the base of her spine fizz like sherbet. 'My only regret is I didn't see you for what you were at the outset. You're a classic chameleon. You can change in the blink of an eye. I had you pegged as an old-fashioned girl who wanted the same things I wanted. But you were not that girl, were you? You were never that girl. You were a harlot on the hunt for sensory adventure and you didn't care where you got it.'

'Why is it such a crime for a woman to want sensory satisfaction?' Eliza asked. 'Why does that make *me* a harlot? What does that make *you?* Why are there no equally derogatory names for men who want to be satisfied physically? Why do women have to feel so bad about their own perfectly natural needs that you men seem to take for granted?'

'What's wrong with your fiancé that he can't give you the satisfaction you want or need?'

The question was like a punch to her chest. 'I'm not prepared to answer that.'

'Does he even exist?'

Eliza looked at him numbly. '*What?*'

'Is he a real person or just someone you made up to use as a get-out-of-jail-free card?' His eyes were hard as they drilled into hers. 'It's a handy device to have a fiancé in the background when you want to get out of an affair that's not going according to plan.'

She swallowed against the lump in her throat. Ewan did exist, but not as he used to be. And it was *her* fault. His life was as good as over. He would never feel the things he used to feel. He could never say the words he used to say. He couldn't even think the thoughts he used to think. He existed…but he didn't. He was caught between the conscious world and the unconscious.

'You're so fiercely loyal to him. But is he as loyal to you?'

Eliza lowered her gaze as she fought her emotions back down. 'He's very loyal. He's a good person. He's always been a good person.'

'You love him.'

She didn't need more than a second to think about it. 'Yes…'

The silence hummed with his bitterness.

How was she going to survive a month of this? What good was going to come out of his attempt to right the wrongs of the past? Nothing could be gained from this encounter. He was intent on revenge but they would both end up even more damaged than they already were. She couldn't fix Ewan and she couldn't fix Leo. She had ruined two lives, three if she counted Samantha.

And what about *her* life—the plans she had made were nothing but pipe dreams now. She wouldn't be able to have the family she wanted. She wouldn't be able to have the love she craved.

She was trapped, just like Ewan was trapped.

Eliza turned to the nursery, desperate to get away from the hatred she could feel pouring out of Leo towards her. 'I'm going to check on Alessandra. She should be awake by now.'

'My daughter's orientation and mobility teacher will

be here at ten,' he said. 'Tatiana works with her until lunchtime twice a week. You can either have that time to yourself or observe some of the things she is helping Alessandra with. I don't expect you to be on duty twenty-four hours a day.'

Eliza looked at him again. 'Aren't you worried that she's going to be upset by my being here for such a short time? It sounds like a lot of people are coming and going in her life. It's no wonder she gets upset and agitated. She doesn't know who is going to walk in the door next.'

'My daughter is used to being managed by carers,' he said. 'It's a fact of life that she will always need to have support around her.'

She held his gaze for a beat that drummed with tension. 'I meant what I said last night. I think you should get Kathleen to call her each day. It will give her something to look forward to and it might make the time go a little quicker for her.'

His jaw seemed to lock for a moment but then he released a harsh-sounding breath. 'I'm not sure if Kathleen will be back. I got an email from her this morning. Her family want her to move back to Ireland. She's still thinking about it. She's going to tell me what she's decided in a couple of weeks' time.'

Eliza swallowed. 'Does that mean you'll want me to stay longer?'

His gaze became steely as it nailed hers. 'Your contract is for one month and one month only. It's not up for negotiation.'

'But what if your daughter wants me to stay?'

'One month.' The words came out clipped through lips pulled tight with tension, those bitter eyes hardening even further. 'That's all I'm prepared to give you.'

'Would you really put your plans for revenge before the interests of your daughter?'

'This is not about revenge.'

She made a sceptical sound in her throat. 'Then what *is* it about?'

His eyes roved her body in a searing sweep that made her skin prickle with heat and longing. The memory of his bruising kiss was still beating beneath the surface of her lips. The need he had awakened was secretly pulsing in the depths of her body—an intense ache that refused to go away. She felt it travel from her core to her breasts as his gaze travelled the length and breadth of her body. 'I think you know what this is about.'

Lust.

It wasn't a word Eliza particularly liked, but how else could she describe how he made her feel? From the very first moment she had met him he had triggered this earthy response in her. She knew he was experienced—*very* experienced. She had come to the relationship with much less experience, but what she had lacked in that department she had more than made up for in passion. Her response to him had shocked her then and it still shocked her now. Didn't that kiss last night prove how dangerous it was to get too close to him? He would dismantle her emotional armour within a heartbeat. Making love with him would unpick every stitch of her carefully constructed resolve. She could not afford to let that happen. Going back to her bleak and lonely life in England would be so much harder to bear if she experienced the mind-blowing pleasure Leo offered. How would she settle for the bitter plate of what fate had dished up to her if she got a taste of such sweet paradise again?

Eliza threw him a contemptuous look born out of the fear that he would somehow see how terrifyingly vulnerable she was to him. 'And just because you want something, you just go out and get it, do you? Well, I've got news for you. I'm not on the market.'

He came up close with that slow, leisurely stroll he had perfected. She refused to back away but instead gave him the full wattage of her heated glare as she steeled herself for the firm grasp of his hands on her arms.

But he didn't.

Instead he gently brushed the back of his bent knuckles down the curve of her cheek in a barely touching caress that totally ambushed her defences. She felt her composure crack as her throat closed over. Tears formed and stung at the back of her eyes. Her chest felt like an oversized balloon was inflating inside it, taking up all the space so her lungs could no longer expand enough to breathe.

'Why are you doing this?' Her voice was not much more than a thread of sound. 'Why now? Why couldn't you have let things be?'

His expression had lost its steely edge and was now almost wistful. 'I wanted to make sure.'

'Sure of…of what?'

'That I didn't make the worst mistake of my life the night you told me you were engaged.'

Eliza swallowed a walnut-sized knot of emotion. 'You…you had a right to be upset…' She couldn't look at him. She lowered her gaze again and stared at her engagement ring instead.

There was the sound of Alessandra waking in the nursery—the rustle of bedclothes and a plaintive wail.

'I'll go to her.' Leo moved past and Eliza listened as he greeted his little daughter. He spoke in Italian but she could hear the love in his voice that was as clear as any translation. '*Buongiorno, tesorina, come ti senti*?'

Was it wrong to wish he could look upon *her* as his treasure too?

CHAPTER SIX

When Eliza came into the nursery Leo had Alessandra in his arms. 'I'll carry her downstairs for you but I won't be able to join you for breakfast,' he said. 'I have an online meeting in a few minutes.'

'Good morning, Alessandra,' Eliza said, reaching out to touch the child's hand that was gripping her father's shirt. 'It looks like we've got a date for breakfast.'

The little girl huddled closer to her father's chest. 'I want to have breakfast with *Papà*.'

Eliza exchanged a brief glance with Leo before addressing the child again. 'I'm afraid that's not possible today. But I'm sure *Papà* will make a special effort to have breakfast with you when he can.'

Alessandra's thin shoulders slumped as she let out a sigh. 'All wight.'

Once Leo had placed his daughter in her high chair in the breakfast room he kissed her on the top of the head and, with a brief unreadable glance at Eliza, he left.

Marella, the housekeeper, came bustling in, cooing to the child in Italian. '*Buongiorno, angioletta mia, tutto bene?*' She turned to Eliza. 'You have to feed her.' She nodded at the food in front of the child. 'She can't do it herself.'

'But surely she's old enough to do some of it on her own?'

'You'll have to discuss that with Signor Valente,' Marella said. 'Kathleen always feeds her. Tatiana, the O and M teacher, is trying to get Alessandra to do more for herself but it's a slow process.'

Eliza settled for a compromise by guiding Alessandra's hands to reach for things on her plate such as pieces of fruit or toast. The little girl was reluctant to drink from anything but her sippy cup so Eliza decided to leave that battle for another day. She knew how important it was to encourage Alessandra to live as normal a life as possible, but pushing her too fast, too soon could be detrimental to her confidence.

Tatiana, the orientation and mobility teacher arrived just as Marella was clearing away the breakfast things. After introducing herself, Tatiana filled Eliza in on the sorts of things she was doing with Alessandra while Marella momentarily distracted Alessandra.

'We're working on her coordination and spatial awareness. A sighted child learns by watching others and trying things for themselves, but a vision-impaired or blind child has no reference point. We have to help them explore the world around them in other ways, by touching and feeling, and by listening and using their sense of smell. We also have to teach what is appropriate behaviour in public, as they don't have the concept of being seen by others.'

'It all sounds rather painstaking,' Eliza said.

'It is,' Tatiana said. 'Alessandra is a bright child but don't let that strong will fool you. When it comes to her exercises she's not well motivated. That is rather typical of a vision-impaired child. They can become rather passive. Our job is to increase her independence little by little.'

'She seems small for her age.'

'Yes, she's on the lower percentile in terms of height and weight, but with more structured exercise she should catch up.'

'Is there anything I can do to help while I have her on my own?'

'Yes, of course,' Tatiana said. 'I'll write out a list of games and activities. You might even think of some of your own. Signor Valente told me you are a teacher, yes?'

'Yes. I teach a primary school class in a community school in London.'

'Then you're perfect for the job,' Tatiana said. 'What a shame you can't be here permanently. Kathleen is a sweetheart but she gives in to Alessandra too easily.'

'The post is only for a month,' Eliza said, automatically fingering the diamond on her left hand. 'I have to get back, in any case.'

'Don't get me wrong,' Tatiana said. 'Leo Valente is a loving father, but like a lot of parents of children with special needs, he is very protective—almost too protective at times. I guess it's hard for him, being a single parent.'

'Did you meet Alessandra's mother before she died?' Eliza asked.

Tatiana's expression said far more than her words. 'Yes and I still can't work out how those two ended up married to each other. I got the impression from Giulia it was a rebound relationship on his part.' She blew out a breath as her gaze went to where Alessandra was sitting in her high chair. 'I bet that's a one-night stand he's regretted ever since.'

Eliza could feel a wave of heat move through her cheeks. *I'm sure it's not the only one,* she thought with a searing pain near her heart. 'Leo loves his daughter. There can be no doubt of that.'

'Yes, of course he does,' Tatiana said. 'But it's probably not the life he envisaged for himself, is it? But then, lots of parents feel the same when they have a child with a disability. It's hard to get specialised nannies. Children with special needs can be very demanding. But to see them reach their potential is very rewarding.'

'Yes, I can imagine it is.'

'At least Signor Valente has the money to get the best help available,' Tatiana said. 'But it's true what people say, isn't it? You can't buy happiness.'

Eliza thought of Leo's brooding personality and the flashes of pain she had glimpsed in his eyes. 'No…you certainly can't…'

The morning passed swiftly as Tatiana worked with Alessandra in structured play with Eliza as active observer. There were shape puzzles for Alessandra to do as well as walking exercises to strengthen her muscles and improve her coordination. The little toddler wasn't good at walking on her own, even while holding someone's hand. Her coordination and muscle strength was significantly poorer compared to children her age. And, of course, what was difficult to the little tot was then wilfully avoided.

Eliza could see how a tired and overburdened parent would give in and do things for their child that they should really be encouraging them to do for themselves. It was draining and exhausting just watching the little girl work through her exercises and, even though Tatiana tried to make the session as playful as possible, Alessandra became very tired towards the end. There was barely time for a few mouthfuls of lunch before she was ready for her nap.

Eliza sat in the anteroom and read a book she had brought with her, keeping an ear out for any sign of the little girl becoming restless. An hour passed and then half of another but the child slept on. She could feel her own eyelids drooping when Marella came to the door with a steaming cup of tea and a freshly baked cup cake on a pretty flowered plate.

'You don't have to stay here like a prison guard.' Marella placed the tea and cake on the little table by Eliza's chair. 'There's a portable monitor. Its range is wide enough to reach the gardens and the pool. Didn't Signor Valente show you?'

'No…I expect he had too many other things on his mind.'

Marella shook her head sadly. 'Poor man. He has too much work to do and too little time to do it. He is always torn. He wants to be a good father but he has a big company to run. He'll drive himself to an early grave just like his father did if he's not careful.'

Eliza lowered her gaze to the cup of tea she was cradling in her hands. She thought of Leo getting through each day, feeling overly burdened and guilty about the competing demands of his life. Who did he turn to when things got a little overwhelming? One of his mistresses? How could someone he was just having sex with help him deal with his responsibilities? *Did* he turn to anyone or did he shoulder it all alone? No wonder he seemed angry and bitter a lot of the time. Maybe it wasn't just *her* that brought out that in him. Maybe he was just trying to cope with what life had thrown at him—just like she was trying to do, with limited success.

'I can imagine it must be very difficult for him, juggling it all.'

'After you've had your tea, why don't you take a

stroll out in the garden?' Marella said. 'I'll listen out for the little one. I'll take the monitor with me. I'll be on this floor in any case. I have to remake the bed the agency girl was using.'

Eliza could think of nothing better than a bit of sunshine. It seemed a long time since she had been in the fresh air. The villa was becoming oppressive, with its forbiddingly long corridors and large gloomy rooms. She put her cup down on the table. 'Are you sure?'

'But of course.' Marella shooed her away. 'It will do you good.'

The sun was deliciously warm as Eliza strolled about the gardens, the scent of roses thick and heady in the air. Was it her knowledge of Alessandra's blindness that made the colours of the roses seem so spectacular all of a sudden? Deep blood reds, soft and bright pinks and crimson, variegated ones, yellow and orange and the snowy perfection of white ones. Even the numerous shades of green in the foliage of the other plants and shrubs stood out to her as she wandered past. She went past the fountain and down a crushed limestone pathway to a grotto that was protected by the shade of a weeping birch. It was a magical sort of setting, secluded and private—the perfect place for quiet reflection. She slipped off her cardigan and sat on the wrought iron bench, wondering how many couples through the centuries had conducted their trysts under the umbrella-like shade of the lush and pendulous branches.

The sound of a footfall on the stones of the pathway made Eliza's heart give a little kick behind her rib-cage. She stood up from the seat just as Leo came into view. He looked just as surprised to see her. She saw the camera-shutter flinch of his features in that nanosecond before he got control and assumed one of his inscrutable expressions.

'Eliza.'

'Marella told me to take a break. She's listening out for Alessandra. She's got the monitor. I didn't know you had one; otherwise—' she knew she was babbling but couldn't seem to stop '—she told me it would be all right and—'

'You're not under lock and key.'

Eliza tried to read his expression but it was like trying to read one of the marble statues she had walked past earlier in the long wide gallery in the villa. She wondered if he had come down here to be alone. Perhaps it was his private place for handling the difficulties of his life. No wonder he resented her presence. She was intruding on his only chance at solitude.

'I'd better head back.' She turned to pick up her cardigan that she'd left on the seat.

'What have you done to your arms?'

'Um—nothing.' She bunched the cardigan against her chest. It was too late to put it back on.

His frown brought his brows to a deep V above his eyes. 'Did I…?' He seemed momentarily lost for words. 'Did I do that to you?'

'It's nothing…really.' She began to turn away but he anchored her with a gentle band of his broad fingers around her wrist.

His touch was like a circle of flame. She felt the shockwave of it right to the secret heart of her. Her skin danced with jittery sensations. Her heart fluttered like a hummingbird and her breath halted in her throat like a horse refusing a jump.

'I'm sorry.' His voice was a deep bass—deeper than organ pipes. It made her spine loosen and quiver. It spoke to the primal woman in her, especially when he ever so gently ran one of his fingers over the marks he had made on her flesh. 'Do they hurt?'

'No, of course not.' She was struggling to deal with her spiralling emotions. Why did he have to stand so close to her? How could she resist him when he was close enough for her to sense his arrantly male reaction to her? If she moved so much as an inch she would feel him.

Oh, how she wanted to feel him!

Could he see how much she ached for him? How desperate she was to have it taken out of her control, to be swept away to a world where nothing mattered but the senses he awakened and satisfied.

'I'd forgotten how very sensitive your skin is.' His fingers danced over her left forearm, leaving every pore screaming for more of his tantalising touch.

Eliza swallowed convulsively. This was going to get out of hand rather rapidly if he kept on with this softly-softly assault on her senses. She could fend him off when he was angry and bitter. She could withstand him—only just—when he was brooding and resentful.

But in this mood he was far more dangerous.

Her need of him was dangerous.

She pulled back from his loose hold but it tightened a mere fraction, keeping her tethered to him—to temptation. 'I…I have to go…' Her words sounded desperate, her breathing even more so. She fought to control herself. She didn't want him to see how close to being undone she was. 'Please…let me go…'

'That was my mistake four years ago.' He brought her even closer, his hands going to the small of her back, pressing her to his need. 'I should never have let you go.'

'It wasn't a mistake.' She tried to push against his chest but he wouldn't budge. 'I had to go. I didn't belong with you. I *don't* belong with you.'

His hands gripped her wrists, gently but firmly. 'You keep fighting me but you want this as much as I do. I know you do. I *know* you want me. I feel it every time you look at me.'

'It's wrong.' Eliza was close to breaking. She couldn't allow herself to fold emotionally. She had to be strong. She had to think of poor Ewan. It was her fault he had been robbed of everything. He would never feel love again. He would never feel passion or desire.

Why should *she* feel it when he no longer could?

'Tell your fiancé you want a break.'

'I can't do that.'

'Why not?'

'He wouldn't understand.'

'Make him understand. Tell him you want a month to have a think about things. Is that so much to ask? For God's sake, you're giving him the rest of your life. What is one measly month in the scheme of things?'

Eliza tried to control her trembling bottom lip. 'Relationships can't be turned on and off like that. I've made a commitment. I can't opt out of it.'

His dark eyes glittered. 'Are saying you can't or you won't?'

She forced herself to hold his challenging look. 'I won't be used by you, Leo.'

One of his hands burned like a brand in the small of her back as he drew her closer. 'What's all this talk of me using you?' His voice was still low and deep, making her resolve fall over like a precariously assembled house of cards. 'You want the same thing I want. There doesn't have to be a winner or a loser in this. We can both have what we want.'

Eliza could feel the slow melt of her bones. She could feel that sharp dart of longing deep inside her body, the need that longed to be assuaged. Was it wrong to want to feel his passionate possession one more time? To explore the intense heat that continued to flare between them? But would one month be enough? How could it *ever* be enough? Experiencing that earth-shattering pleasure again would only leave her frustrated and miserable for the rest of her life. She would always be thinking of him, aching for him, *missing* him. It had been hard enough four years ago. He had lived in her body for all this time, making her even more restless and unhappy with her lot in life.

But it *was* her lot in life.

There was no escaping the fact that Ewan's life had been destroyed and that she had been the one to do it. How could she carry on with her life as if it didn't matter?

Of course it mattered.

It would always matter.

With a strength Eliza had no idea she possessed, she pushed back from him. 'I'm sorry…' She moved away from him until she was almost standing in the shrubbery. 'You're asking too much. It's all been too much. Finding out about your daughter's blindness… seeing how hard it is for her and for you. I can't think straight…I'm confused and upset…'

'You need more time.'

She squeezed her eyes closed for a moment as if that would make all of this go away. But when she opened them again he was still standing there, looking at her with his unwavering gaze.

'It's not about time…' She bit down on her lower lip. 'It's just not our time…' *It was never our time.*

He tucked a loose strand of her hair behind her ear. Her skin shivered at his tender touch, the nerves pirouetting beneath the surface until she was almost dizzy with longing. 'I've handled this appallingly, haven't I?' he asked, resting that same hand on the nape of her neck.

Eliza wasn't sure how to answer so remained silent. His hand was strong and yet gentle—protective. She longed to be held by him and never let go. But the past—their past—was a yawning canyon that was too wide and deep to cross.

He let out a rough-sounding sigh and, stepping away from her to look out over the rear garden, that same hand that had moments ago caressed her was now rubbing at the back of his neck as if trying to ease giant knots of tension buried there. 'I'm still not sure why I came to you that day in London. I needed a nanny in a hurry and for some reason the first person I thought of was you.' His hand dropped to his side as he turned and looked at her again. 'But maybe it was because I wanted you to see what my life had become.' His expression was tortured with anguish and frustration. 'I've got more money than I know what to do with and yet I can't fix my child. I can't *make* her see.'

Eliza felt his frustration. It was imbedded in every word he had spoken. It was in every nuance of his expression. He was in pain for his daughter—physical and emotional pain. 'You're a wonderful father, Leo. Your role is to love and provide for her. You're doing all that and more.'

'She needs more than I can give her.' He dragged a hand over his face. It pulled at his features, distorting them, making him seem older than his years. 'She needs her mother. But that's another thing I can't fix. I can't bring her mother back.'

'That's not your fault. You mustn't blame yourself.'

He gave her a weary look. 'Giulia was already broken when I met her. But I probably made it a thousand times worse.'

'How did you meet her?'

'In a bar.'

Eliza felt her face colour up. 'Not a great place to find lasting love…'

He gave her a look she couldn't quite decipher. 'No, but then people at a crossroads in their lives often hang out in bars. I was no different than Giulia. We'd both been disappointed in love. She'd been let down by a long-term lover. In hindsight, I would have been much better served—and her, for that matter—if I'd just listened to what had been going on in her life. She needed a friend, not a new lover to replace the one she'd lost.'

'What happened?'

His gaze dropped to the gravel at his feet as he kicked absently at a loose pebble. 'We had a one-night stand.' His eyes met hers again. 'I know you might find this hard to believe, but I don't make a habit of them. I regretted it as soon as it was over. We had no real chemistry. In some ways I think she only went through with it because she wanted to prove something to herself—that she could sleep with another man after being with her lover for so long.' He took a breath and slowly released it. 'She called me a month later and told me she was pregnant.'

'You must have been furious.'

He shrugged one shoulder. 'I wasn't feeling anything much at that stage. I guess that's why I offered to marry her. I truly didn't care either way. As far as I was concerned, the only woman I wanted wasn't available. What did it matter who I married?'

Eliza ignored the flash of pain his words evoked and frowned at him. 'Why was marriage so important to you? Most men your age are quite content with having affairs. They wouldn't dream of settling down with one person for the rest of their life, even when there is a child involved, especially one that wasn't planned.'

'My father loved my mother,' he said. 'It ended badly, but he always instilled in me that it was worth committing to one person. He didn't believe in half measures. His philosophy was you were either in or you were out. I admired that in him.

'I tried my best with Giulia. I gave her what I could but it wasn't enough. At the end of the day we didn't love each other. No amount of commitment on my part could compensate for her guilt over Alessandra's blindness. She just couldn't handle it. She rejected her right from the start. In her mind, it was as if someone had handed her the wrong baby in the hospital. She couldn't seem to accept that this was what life was going to be like from now on.'

'I'm sure there are a lot of parents who feel that way,' Eliza said.

He scored a pathway through his hair, as if even thinking about that time in his life made his head ache. 'The thing was, Giulia didn't want to have *my* baby. She wanted her ex's child.'

Eliza's frown showed her confusion as it pulled at

her forehead. 'But you said she deliberately set out to get pregnant, that she set you up.'

He gave her another weary look. 'It's true. But the thing is, I could have been anyone that night. She wanted to hit out at the man who'd let her down so badly. She wasn't thinking straight. On another night she might not have done it, but of course once it was done it was too late to undo it. She wasn't the type to have an abortion and, to be honest, I didn't want her to. We were both responsible for what happened. I could have walked away from her that night. But, in a way, I think I was trying to prove something too.'

Eliza sank her teeth into her lip, thinking about how devastating all this had been for him. His life had changed so swiftly and so permanently. And *she* had been part of that devastation when she had rejected his proposal. Was she always destined to ruin other people's lives? To make them desperately unhappy and destroy the life they had envisaged for themselves?

'I'm sorry…I can see now why you feel I'm partly to blame for how things have turned out. But who's to say we would've had a great relationship if I had been free to marry you?'

His dark eyes meshed with hers. 'Do you seriously doubt that we couldn't have had a satisfying relationship after what we shared during those three weeks?'

She turned away from his penetratingly hot gaze and folded her arms across her middle, cupping her elbows with her crossed over hands. 'There's much more to a relationship than sex. There's companionship and emotional honesty and closeness. The best sex in the world doesn't make up for those things.'

HARLEQUIN® READER SERVICE—Here's How It Works:

Accepting your 2 free books and 2 free gifts (gifts valued at approximately $10.00) places you under no obligation to buy anything. You may keep the books and gifts and return the shipping statement marked "cancel". If you do not cancel, about a month later we'll send you 6 additional books and bill you just $4.30 each for the regular-print edition or $5.05 each for the larger-print edition in the U.S. or $4.99 each for the regular-print edition or $5.49 each for the larger-print edition in Canada. That's a savings of at least 14% off the cover price. It's quite a bargain! Shipping and handling is just 50¢ per book in the U.S. and 75¢ per book in Canada.* You may cancel at any time, but if you choose to continue, every month we'll send you 6 more books, which you may either purchase at the discount price or return to us and cancel your subscription.

*Terms and prices subject to change without notice. Prices do not include applicable taxes. Sales tax applicable in N.Y. Canadian residents will be charged applicable taxes. Offer not valid in Quebec. All orders subject to credit approval. Credit or debit balances in a customer's account(s) may be offset by any other outstanding balance owed by or to the customer. Please allow 4 to 6 weeks for delivery. Offer available while quantities last.

If offer card is missing write to: Harlequin Reader Service, P.O. Box 1867, Buffalo NY

NO POSTAGE NECESSARY IF MAILED IN THE UNITED STATES

BUSINESS REPLY MAIL

FIRST-CLASS MAIL PERMIT NO. 717 BUFFALO, NY

POSTAGE WILL BE PAID BY ADDRESSEE

HARLEQUIN READER SERVICE
PO BOX 1867
BUFFALO NY 14240-9952

'Is that what you have with your fiancé? Emotional closeness?'

'I should get back…' Eliza glanced towards the villa. 'Alessandra will be well and truly awake by now. Marella will be wondering what's happened to me.'

She started back along the pathway but she didn't hear Leo following her. She glanced back when she got to the fountain but he had disappeared from sight. She gave an uneven sigh and, with a little slump of her shoulders, made her way inside the villa.

CHAPTER SEVEN

ALESSANDRA HAD ONLY just woken when Eliza came back to the nursery. 'I've got a special surprise in store,' she said as she lifted her out of the cot.

'What is it?' Alessandra asked, rubbing at one of her eyes.

Tatiana had explained to Eliza that eye-rubbing was something a lot of vision-impaired children did. But while it gave temporary comfort similar to sucking a thumb, as the child got older it was less socially acceptable. Tatiana had advised that distracting the child from the habit was the best way to manage it, so Eliza gently pulled her hand away and circled her tiny palm with the finger play, *Ring a Ring o' Roses.*

Alessandra giggled delightedly. 'Do it again.'

'Give me your other hand.'

The little girl held out her hand and Eliza repeated the rhyme, her heart squeezing as she saw the unadulterated joy on the toddler's face. 'Again! Again!'

'Maybe later,' Eliza said. 'I have other plans for you, young lady. We're going for a walk.'

'I don't want to walk. Carry me.'

'No carrying today, little Munchkin,' Eliza said. 'You've got two lovely little legs. You need to learn to use them a bit more.'

She took the little tot's hand and led her out to the landing and then down the stairs. She got Alessandra to feel the balustrade as she went down and to plant her feet carefully on each step before taking another. It was a slow process but well worth it as by the time they got down to the ground floor she could tell Alessandra was a little more confident.

'Now we're going to go outside to the garden,' Eliza said. 'Have you been out there much?'

'Kathleen used to take me sometimes but then she got stinged by a bee. I cried because I thought it was going to sting me too.'

'Don't worry; I won't let you get stung.' Eliza gave the little child's hand a gentle squeeze of reassurance. 'There's a lot of lovely things to smell and feel out there. Flowers are some of the most beautiful things in nature but the really cool thing is you don't have to see them to appreciate them. Lots of them have really lovely perfumes, particularly roses. I bet after a while you'll be able to tell them apart, just from smelling them.'

Once they were out in the garden, Eliza led Alessandra down to one of the rose gardens. She picked some blooms and held them to the child's little nose, smiling as Alessandra sniffed and smiled in turn. 'Beyootiful!' she said.

'That's a deep red one,' Eliza said. 'It's got a really rich scent. Here's a bright pink one. Its scent is a little less intense. What do you think?'

Alessandra pushed her nose against the velvet bloom. 'Nice.'

'Feel the petals,' Eliza said. 'There aren't any thorns on this one. I checked.'

The little girl fingered the soft petals, discovering each fold, her face full of concentration as if she was trying to picture what she was feeling. 'Can I smell some more?'

'Of course.' Eliza picked a yellow one this time. 'This one reminds me of the sunshine. It's bright and cheerful with a light, fresh fragrance.'

'Mmm.' Alessandra breathed in the fragrance. 'But I like the first one best.'

'That was the red one.' Eliza put them in a row on the ground and got Alessandra to sit on the grass beside her. 'Let's play a game. I'm going to hand you a rose and you have to tell me which colour it is by the smell. Do you think you can do that?'

'Will I know my colours after this?'

Eliza looked at the tiny tot's engaging little face and felt her heart contract. 'I think you're going to be an absolute star at this game. Now, here goes. Which one is this?'

Leo was coming back from speaking to one of the gardeners working on a retaining wall at the back of the garden when he saw Eliza and his little daughter sitting in a patch of sunshine on the lawn near the main rose garden. Eliza's attention was focused solely on Alessandra. She was smiling and tickling his daughter's nose with a rose. Alessandra was giggling in delight. The tinkling bell sound of his little girl's laughter sounded out across the garden. It was the most wonderful sound he had ever heard. It made something that had been stiff and locked inside his chest for years loosen.

He watched as Eliza rained a handful of rose petals from above Alessandra's head. Alessandra reached up and caught some of them, crushing them to her face and giggling anew.

He could have stood there and watched them for hours.

But then, as if Eliza had suddenly sensed his presence, she turned her head and the remaining petals in her hand dropped to the lawn like confetti.

He closed the distance in a few strides and his little daughter also turned her head in his direction as she heard him approach. '*Papà*?'

'You look like you are having a lot of fun, *mia piccola*.'

'I know my colours!' she said excitedly. 'Eliza's been teaching me.'

Leo quirked one of his brows at Eliza. 'You look like you're enjoying yourself too.'

'Alessandra is a very clever little girl,' she said. 'She's a joy to teach. Now, Alessandra, I'm going to pick some more roses. Let's show *Papà* how clever you are at distinguishing which one is which.'

Leo watched as she picked a handful of roses and came back to sit on the lawn next to his daughter. Alessandra's expression was a picture to behold. She held up her face for the brush of each velvet rose against her little nose. She breathed deeply and, after thinking about it for a moment, proudly announced, 'That's the pink one!'

'Very good,' Eliza said. 'Now, how about this one?'

'It's the red one!'

Leo looked on in amazement. How had she done it? It was like a miracle. His little daughter was able to tell each rose from the others on the basis of its smell but somehow Eliza had got her to associate the colour as well. Even though, strictly speaking, Alessandra hadn't learned her colours at all, it was a way to make her distinguish them by another route. It was nothing less than a stroke of genius. He felt incredibly touched that Eliza had taken the trouble to work her way through a task that had seemed insurmountable so that his little girl could feel more normal.

'OK, now, how about this one?' Eliza held up a white one and Alessandra sniffed and sniffed, her little face screwing up in confusion.

'It's not the yellow one, is it? It smells different.'

'You clever, clever girl!' Eliza said. 'It's a white one. I tried to trick you, but you're too clever by half. Well done.'

Alessandra was grinning from ear to ear. 'I like this game.'

Leo looked down at Eliza's warm smile. It made that stiff part of his chest loosen another notch. He imagined her with her own child—how natural she would be, how loving and nurturing. It wasn't just the trained teacher in her, either. He was starting to realise it was an essential part of her nature. She genuinely loved children and wanted to bring out the best in them. No wonder she had been recognised as a teacher of excellence. She cared about their learning and achievement. He could see the joy and satisfaction on her face as she worked with Alessandra. Sure, he was paying her big money to do it, but he suspected it wasn't the money that motivated her at all.

Why couldn't *she* have been Alessandra's mother?

'You're scarily good at this game,' Eliza said. 'I'll have to be on my toes to think of new ones to challenge you.' She got to her feet and took one of Alessandra's hands in hers. 'We'd better get you inside, out of this hot sun. I don't want you to get sunburnt.'

Leo moved forward to scoop his daughter up to carry her back to the villa but she seemed content to walk, albeit gingerly, by Eliza's side. He watched as she toddled alongside Eliza, her little hand entwined with hers, her footsteps awkward and cautious, but, with Eliza's gentle encouragement, she gradually gained a little more confidence.

'Four steps, Alessandra,' Eliza said as they got to the flagstone steps leading to the back entrance of the villa. 'Do you want to count them as we go?'

'One…two…three…four!'

Eliza ruffled her hair with an affectionate hand. 'What did I tell you? You're an absolute star. You'll soon be racing about the place without any help at all.'

Marella appeared from the kitchen as they came in. 'I've been baking your favourite cookies, Alessandra. Why don't we let Papà and Eliza have a moment while we have a snack?'

'*Grazie*, Marella,' Leo said. 'There are a few things I'd like to talk to Eliza about. Give us ten minutes.'

'*Sì, signor.*'

Leo met Eliza's gaze once the housekeeper had left with his daughter. 'It seems I was right in selecting you as a suitable stand-in for Kathleen. You've achieved much more in a day with Alessandra than she has in months.'

'I'm sure Kathleen is totally competent as a nanny.'

'That is true, but you seem to have a natural affinity with Alessandra.'

'She's a lovely child.'

'Most of the people who deal with her find her difficult.'

'She has a disability,' she said. 'It's easy to focus on what she can't do, but in my experience in teaching difficult children it is wiser to focus on what they *can* do. She can do a lot more than you probably realise.'

A frown pulled at his brow. 'Are you saying I'm holding her back in some way?'

'No, of course not,' she said. 'You're doing all the right things. It's just that it's sometimes hard to see what she needs from a parent's perspective. You want to protect her but in protecting her you may end up limiting her. She has to experience life. She has to experience the dangers and the disappointments; otherwise she will always live in a protective bubble that has no relation to the real world. She needs to live in the real world. She's blind but that doesn't mean she can't live a fulfilled and satisfying life.'

He moved to the other side of the room, his hand going to his neck, where a golf ball of tension was gnawing at him. 'What do you suggest I do that I'm not already doing?'

'You could spend more time with her, one on one. She needs quality time with you but also quantity time.'

Guilt prodded at him. He knew he wasn't as hands on as he could be. No one had played with him as a child. His mother had been too busy pursuing her own interests while his father had worked long hours to try and keep his company from going under. Leo wanted to be a better parent than his had been, but Alessandra's blindness made him feel so wretchedly inadequate. It had paralysed him as a parent. What if he did or said the wrong thing? What if he upset her or made her feel guilty for having special needs? Giulia, in her distress, had said unforgivable things in the hearing of Alessandra. He had tried to make up for it, but there were times when he wondered if it was already too late.

'I'll try to free up some time,' he said. 'It's hard when I'm trying to juggle a global business. I can't always be here. I have to rely on others to take care of her.'

'You could take her with you occasionally,' she said. 'It would be good for her.'

'What would be the point?' He threw her a frustrated glance. 'She can't *see* anything.'

'No, but she can feel, and she would be with you more than she is now. You are all she has now. The bond she has with you is what will build her confidence and sustain her through life. Stop feeling guilty. It's not your fault she's blind. It wasn't Giulia's fault. It's just what happened. Those were the cards you were dealt. You have to accept that.'

'You're not a parent. You know nothing of the guilt a parent feels.'

Her eyes flinched as if he had struck her. 'I know much more about guilt than you realise. I live with it every day. I *agonise* over it. But does it change anything? No. That's life. You have to find a way to deal with it.' Her gaze fell away from his as she pushed back a strand of her hair off her face.

Leo frowned as he narrowed his gaze to her left hand. 'Where's your ring?'

She glanced down at her hand and her face blanched. 'I don't know…' She looked up at him in panic, her eyes wide with alarm. 'It was there earlier. I have to find it. It's not mine.'

'What do you mean, it's not yours?'

She shifted her gaze again, her demeanour agitated. 'It's my fiancé's mother's. It's a family heirloom. I have to find it. It must have slipped off somewhere. It's a bit loose. I should've had it adjusted, but I—'

'It's probably in the garden where you were playing with Alessandra,' he said. 'I'll go and have a look.'

'I'll come with you,' she said, almost pushing him out of the way in her haste to get out of the door. 'I have to find it.'

'One of the gardeners will pick it up if it's out there,'

Leo said. 'Stop panicking. It didn't look all that valuable.'

She met his gaze with her distressed one. 'It's not about the monetary value. Why does everything have to be about money to you? It's got enormous sentimental value. I can't lose it. I just can't. I have to find it.'

'I trust my staff to hand it in if they find it. You don't have to worry. No one is going to rush it off to the nearest pawn shop.'

Her brow was a fine map of worried lines. 'You don't understand. I have to find it. I don't feel right without it on my finger.'

He grasped her flailing hand and held it firm. 'Why? Because you need it there as a reminder, don't you? Your fiancé is thousands of miles away but without that ring there to prod your conscience you could so easily forget all about him, couldn't you?'

She pulled out of his hold and dashed out of the room. Leo heard the slapping of her flat shoes along the marbled floor.

He followed at a much slower pace.

He would be perfectly happy if the blasted ring was *never* found.

Eliza looked everywhere but there was no sign of her ring. She went over every patch of the lawn. She went over the rose beds and the pathways but there was no trace of it anywhere. Her rising panic beat a sickening tattoo in her chest. How would she explain it to Samantha? It was so careless of her to have neglected to get it tightened. How would she ever make it up to her? It wasn't just any old ring. It was a symbol of Samantha's lifelong love for her husband Geoff and now *she* had lost it.

Leo had come out and spoken to the gardener before he joined her. 'Any sign?'

Eliza shook her head, her stomach still churning in anguish. 'Samantha will be devastated.'

'Samantha?'

'My fiancé's mother.' She wrung her hands, her eyes scanning the lawn in the vain hope that the sunlight would pick up the glitter of the ring. 'I don't know how I'll ever tell her. I have to find it. I *have* to.'

'The gardener will keep on looking. You should come indoors. You look like you're beginning to catch the sun.'

Eliza glanced at her bare arms. They were indeed a little pink in spite of the sunscreen she had put on earlier. She suddenly felt utterly exhausted. Losing the ring was the last straw on top of everything else. That telltale ache had started deep inside her chest. The tears were not far away. She could feel them burning like peroxide behind her eyes. She put her hand up and pinched the bridge of her nose to try and stop them from spilling.

'*Cara*.' Leo put a gentle hand on her shoulder. 'You're getting yourself in such a state. It's just a ring. It can be replaced.'

She shrugged off his hold and glared up at him with burning resentment. 'That's just *so* typical of you, isn't it? If you lose something you just walk out and get a new one. That's what you did when you lost me, wasn't it? You just went right on out and picked up someone else to replace me as soon as you could.'

The garden seemed to go into a stunned silence after her outburst. Even the light breeze that had been teasing the leaves on the trees had suddenly stilled, as if in shock at the bitterness of her words.

Eliza bit her lip as she lowered her gaze. 'I'm sorry…

That was wrong of me. You had a perfect right to move on with your life…'

There was another tense beat of silence.

'I hope you find your ring.' He gave her a curt nod and turned and strode across the lawn, back past the fountain until finally he disappeared out of sight.

CHAPTER EIGHT

WHEN ELIZA CAME downstairs after putting Alessandra to bed there was an envelope with her name on it propped up on the kitchen counter.

'That's your ring,' Marella said as she came out of the pantry. 'Signor Valente found it in the grotto. He was out there for ages looking for it.'

'That was…kind of him…' Eliza fingered the ring through the paper of the envelope. 'I think I'd better get it tightened before I wear it again.'

Marella cocked her head at her as she picked up a cleaning cloth. 'How long have you been engaged to this fiancé of yours?'

'Um…since I was nineteen…eight years.'

'It's a long time.'

She shifted her gaze from the penetrating black ink of the housekeeper's. 'Yes…yes, it is…'

'You're not in love with him, *sì*?'

'I *love* him.' Had she answered *too* quickly? Had she sounded *too* defensive? 'I've always loved him.'

'That's not the same thing as being in love,' Marella said. 'I see how you are with Signor Valente and him with you. He stirs something in you. Something you've tried for a long time to suppress, *sì*?'

Eliza felt a wave of colour wash over her cheeks. 'I'm just the replacement nanny. I'll be gone in four weeks.'

Marella gave the counter top a slow wipe as she mused, 'I wonder if he will let you go.'

'I'm absolutely certain Signor Valente will be enormously pleased to see the back of me,' Eliza said with feeling.

Marella stopped wiping and gave her a level look. 'I wasn't talking about Signor Valente.'

A telling silence slipped past.

'Excuse me…' Eliza forced a polite smile that felt more like a grimace. 'I have to check on Alessandra.'

When Eliza came downstairs an hour later Marella was just leaving to attend a family function.

'There is a meal all set up on gas flamed warmers in the dining room,' she said as she tied a nylon scarf around her neck. 'I think Signor Valente is in the study. Will you be all right to handle dishing up? Don't worry about clearing up afterwards. I can do that in the morning.'

'I wouldn't dream of leaving a mess for you to face in the morning,' Eliza said. 'I'm perfectly capable of dishing up and clearing away. Have a good evening.'

'*Grazie*.'

Eliza glanced towards the study once the housekeeper had left. Should she wait until Leo came out for dinner to thank him for finding her ring or should she seek him out now? She was still deciding when the door suddenly opened.

He saw her hovering there and arched a brow. 'Did you want me?'

I want you. I want you. I want you. It was like a chant inside her head but it was reverberating throughout her body as well. She could feel that on-off pulse deep in her core intensifying the longer his dark, mesmerising gaze held hers.

'Um…I wanted to thank you for finding my ring,' she said, knowing her cheeks were burning fiery red. 'It was very thoughtful of you to take the time to keep looking.'

'It was behind the seat in the grotto. You must've lost it when you picked up your cardigan.' His dark gaze glinted satirically. 'I'm surprised you didn't notice it missing earlier.'

Eliza set her mouth. 'Yes, well, I'm going to get it tightened so it doesn't happen again.'

He reached for her hand before she could step away. She sucked in a breath as those long, strong, tanned fingers imprisoned hers. Her heart started a madcap rhythm behind her breastbone and her skin tingled and tightened all over. 'W…what are you doing?' Was that her voice, that tiny mouse-like squeak of sound?

His gaze went to her mouth, lingering there. She felt her lips soften and part slightly, her response to him as automatic as breathing. His fingers were warm and dry around hers. She imagined them on other parts of her body, how it had felt to have them caress her intimately, her breasts, her inner thighs, the feminine heart of her that had swelled and flowered under his spine-tingling touch. Her insides clenched with longing as she thought of the stroke of his tongue against her—that most intimate of all kisses. How he had seemed to know from their first time together what she needed to reach fulfilment.

She could see the memory of it in his gaze as it came back to mesh with hers. It made her spine shiver to see that silent message pass between them…the universal language of making love.

Passionate, primal—primitive.

'*Ho voglia di te—ti voglio adesso.*' His words were like a verbal caress, all the more powerfully, intoxicatingly stimulating as they were delivered in his mother tongue.

Eliza swallowed as her heart raced with excitement. 'I don't understand what you just said…' *But I've got a pretty fair idea!*

Those dark eyes glittered with carnal intent as he grasped her by the hips and, with a little jerk forwards, he locked her against his erection. She felt it against her belly, the thunder of his blood mimicking the sensual cyclone that was happening within her own body. Her breasts ached for his touch. She could feel them swelling against the lace constraints of her bra. Her mouth tingled in anticipation of his covering it, plundering it. She sent the tip of her tongue out to moisten the surface of her lips. Her need of him was consuming her common sense like galloping, greedy flames did to a little pile of tinder-dry toothpicks.

'I want you—I want you now.' He said it this time in English and it had exactly the same devastatingly sensual impact.

'I want you too.' It was part confession, part plea.

He splayed a hand through her hair, gripping her almost roughly as his mouth came down on hers. It was a kiss that spoke of desperate longing, of needs that had for too long gone unmet, of a man wanting a woman so badly he could barely control his primitive response to her. It thrilled Eliza to feel that level of desire in him because it so completely and so utterly matched her own.

The stroke and glide of his tongue against hers set

her senses aflame. She undulated her hips against him, whimpering in delight as he in turn growled deep in his throat and responded by pressing even harder against her.

His hands moved over her body, skating over her breasts, leaving them tingling and twitching in their wake. She wanted more. When had she not wanted more from him? She wanted to feel his hands on her, flesh-to-flesh, to feel their skin in warm and sensual contact.

Her hands went to the front of his shirt, pulling at it as if it was nothing but a sheet of paper covering him. Buttons popped and a seam tore but she didn't hold back. Her mouth went to every bit of hard muscled flesh she uncovered. From the dish at the base of his neck just below his Adam's apple, down his sternum, taking a sideways detour to his flat dark male nipples, rolling the tip of her tongue over them in turn, before going lower in search of his belly button and beyond.

'Wait.' The one word command was rough and low. 'Ladies first.'

A shiver ran over her. She knew what he was going to do. The anticipation of it, the memory of it made her legs tremble like leaves in a wind tunnel.

He picked her up in his arms, carrying her effortlessly to the sofa inside his study. She felt the soft press of the cushions as he laid her down, those dark eyes holding hers with the unmistakable message of their sensual purpose, thrilling her from her tingling scalp to her curling toes.

He came back over her, but only to shove her dress above her hips. One of his hands peeled off her knickers, the slow but deliberate trail of lace as he pulled them down over her thigh to her ankles, another masterstroke of seduction in his considerable arsenal. She kicked off the lace along with her shoes, snatching in a quick breath as he bent his head to the swollen heart of her.

The intimacy of it should have appalled her given the current context of their relationship, but somehow it didn't. It felt completely natural for him to be touching her like this. To be touching and stroking her body as if it were the most fascinating and delicately fragrant flower he had ever seen.

'You are *so* beautiful.'

Oh, those words were like a symphony written only for her! She didn't feel beautiful with anyone else. No one else could make her body sing with such perfect harmony the way he did.

He took his time, ramping up her arousal to the point where she was sure she was going to scream if he didn't give her that final stroke that would send her careening into oblivion.

'Please...*oh, please...*' The words came out part groan, part gasp.

'Say you want me.'

'I want you. I want you.' She was panting as if she had just run up a steep incline. 'I want you.'

'Tell me you want me like no other man.'

She dug her fingers like claws into the cushioned sofa, her hips bucking as he continued his sensual torture. 'I want you more than anyone else... Oh, God. *Oh, God...*' Her orgasm splintered her senses into a starburst of feeling. It rattled and shook her body like a ragdoll in a madman's hands. It went on and on until she finally came out the other side, limbless and spent and breathless.

Leo moved up her body and set to work on removing her dress and bra. Eliza lifted her arms up like a child as he uncovered her flesh. She sighed with bone-deep pleasure as he took her breasts in his hands.

How had she gone so long without this exquisite worship of her body? Her flesh was alive with intense feeling. Shivers were still cascading down her spine like a waterfall of champagne bubbles. The very hairs on her head were still dancing on tiptoe. Her inner core was still pulsating with the aftershocks of the cataclysmic eruption of ecstasy that had rippled through it.

His hands gripped her hips once more as his body reared over hers. Somehow he'd had the foresight to apply a condom. She vaguely recalled him retrieving one from his wallet in his back pocket before he had shucked his trousers off.

He kissed her again, his mouth hard and yet soft in turn. It was a devastatingly seductive technique, yet another one he had mastered to perfection. She felt his erection poised for entry against her. She opened her legs for him, welcoming him with one of her hands pressed to the taut and carved curve of his buttocks, the other behind his head, pulling his mouth back down to hers as her ankles hooked around his legs.

He surged into her with a groan that came from deep at the back of his throat. It bordered on a rougher than normal entry but she welcomed it with a groan of pleasure. He seemed to check himself and then started to move a little more slowly, but she pushed him to increase his pace with little encouraging gasps and whimpers and further pressure from her hands pressing down on his buttocks.

She felt the rocking motion of his body within hers. She heard the intervals of his breathing gradually increase. She felt the tension in his muscles as they bunched up under the caress of her hands. The friction of his body within hers sent off her senses into another tailspin of anticipatory delight.

But still he wasn't intent on his own pleasure.

He was still focused on bringing about another delicious wave of hers and brought his fingers down to touch her. The way he seemed to know how much pressure and friction she needed to maximise her pleasure was the final undoing of her. The continued thrusting of his body and the delicate but magical ministration of his fingers were an earth-shattering combination. She was catapulted into another crazily spinning vortex of feeling that robbed her of all sense of time and place.

It was all feeling—feeling that was centred solely in her body.

But as she was coming down from the heights of human pleasure her mind resumed enough focus to register his powerful release. It sent another shockwave of pleasure through her body. She had felt every moment of that powerful pumping surge as he lost himself. There was something about that total loss of control that moved her deeply. It had always been this way between them. A mind-blowing combustion of lust and longing, and yet something else that was less easily definable…

As she moved her hands to the front of his body she noticed the pale circle on her bare left ring finger. It was a stark reminder of her commitment elsewhere.

Her stomach sank in despair.

She wasn't free.

She wasn't free.

She pushed against his chest without meeting his gaze. 'I want to get up.'

He held her down with a gentle but firm press of his hand on her left shoulder. 'Not so fast, *cara*. What's wrong?'

Eliza couldn't look at him. *Wouldn't* look at him. She stared at the peppery stubble on the bulge of his Adam's apple instead. 'This should never have happened.'

He took her chin between his finger and thumb and forced her to meet his gaze. 'Why is that?'

Her eyes smarted with the tears she resolved she *would not* shed in front of him. 'How can you *ask* that?'

His gaze quietly assessed hers. 'You still feel guilty about the natural impulses you have always felt around me?'

She lowered her lashes, chewing at her lip until she tasted the metallic sourness of blood. 'They might be natural but they're not appropriate.'

'Because you're still intent on tying yourself to a man who can't give you what you want or need?'

She continued to valiantly squeeze back the tears, still not looking at him. 'Please, let's not go over this again. I'm here with you now. I'm doing what you asked and paid me to do. Please don't ask me to do any more than that.'

He released a gusty sigh and got up, dressing again with an economy of movement Eliza privately envied. She felt exposed, not just physically—even though she had somehow managed to drag her discarded dress over her nakedness—but emotionally, and that was far more terrifying.

'Contrary to what you might think, I didn't pay you to sleep with me.' His voice was deep and rough, the words sounding as if they had been dragged along a gravel pathway. 'That is entirely separate from your position here as nanny to my daughter.'

She gave him a pointed look. 'Both are temporary appointments, are they not?'

His eyes were deep and dark and unfathomable. 'That depends.'

'Is Kathleen coming back?'

'She hasn't yet decided.'

'I thought you said my month-long contract was not up for negotiation,' Eliza said with a little frown. 'If she decides not to return, does that mean you'll offer me the post?'

'That also depends.'

She arched her brow. 'On what?'

'On whether you want to stay longer.'

Eliza chewed at her lip. If things had been different, of course she would stay. She would live with him as his lover, as his mistress, his daughter's nanny—whatever he wanted, she would do it because she wanted him so much.

But things *weren't* different.

They were exactly the same as they had been four years ago. It didn't matter what she wanted. It was the shackles of her guilt that would always make her forfeit what she wanted. How could she stay here with Leo and leave her other life behind? It was a fanciful dream she had to erase from her mind, just as she'd had to do in the past.

Eliza thought of little Alessandra, of how attached the child had become to her in such a short time. It wasn't just that the little girl was looking for a mother substitute. Eliza had latched onto her with equal measure. She looked forward to their time together. She felt excited about the ways in which Alessandra was growing and developing in confidence and independence. It wasn't just the teacher in her that was being validated, either. It was the deep-seated maternal instinct in her that longed to be expressed. Alessandra was responding to that strong instinct in her to love and protect and nurture.

If things were different, *she* would have been Alessandra's mother.

There was still a fiendish pain inside her chest at the thought of another woman sharing that deeply bonding experience with Leo. She so desperately wanted to be a mother. Each birthday that passed was a painful, gut-twisting reminder of her dream slipping even further out of her grasp.

Eliza brought her gaze back to his once she was sure she had her emotions hidden behind a mask of composure. 'Staying longer isn't an option…'

'Driving up the price, are we, Eliza?' A ripple of tension appeared along his jaw, his dark eyes flashing at her with disgust. 'That's what you're doing, isn't it? You want me to pay you a little extra to stay on as my mistress. How much do you want? Have you got a figure in mind?'

She took a steadying breath against the blast of his anger and turned away. 'There's no point talking to you in this mood.'

A hard hand came down on her forearm and turned her back to face him. His eyes blazed with heated purpose. She felt it ignite a fire in her blood where his fingers were wrapped around her wrist like a convict iron.

The tension in the air crackled like sheet lightning over a wide open plain.

'Don't turn away from me when I'm speaking to you,' he rasped.

Her chin went up and her eyes shot him their own fiery glare. 'Don't order me about like a child.'

His dark eyes glinted menacingly as they warred with hers. 'I'm paying you to obey my orders, damn it.'

Eliza felt a trail of molten heat roll down her spine but still her chin went even higher. 'You're not paying me enough to bow and scrape to you like a simpering servant.'

Those fingers burned her flesh like a brand. That hard-muscled body tempted her like an irresistible lure. Those dark eyes wrestled with hers until every nerve in her body was jangling and tingling with sensual hunger.

Heat exploded between her legs.

She could almost feel him there, that pounding surge of his body that triggered something raw and earthy and deeply primitive inside her.

'How much?' His eyes smouldered darkly. 'How much to have you in my bed for the rest of the month? How much to have you bowing and scraping and simpering to my every need?'

A reckless demon made her goad him. 'You can't afford me.'

'Try me. I have my limit. If you go over it I'll soon tell you.'

Eliza thought of the small house where Ewan and his mother lived in Suffolk. She thought of how much the bathroom needed renovating to make showering him easier for Samantha. She thought of the heating that needed improving because Ewan, as a quadriplegic, had no way of controlling his own body temperature. And then there were the lifting and toileting and feeding aids that always seemed to need an upgrade.

It all cost an astonishing amount of money.

Money Leo Valente was willing to pay her to be his mistress for the rest of the month.

Her heart tapped out an erratic tattoo. Maybe if she took the money it would make her feel less guilty about sleeping with him while she was engaged to Ewan. It would make it impossible to treat their relationship as anything but a business deal.

Well, perhaps not impossible…but unlikely.

He would have her body but she wouldn't sell him her heart.

Eliza met his hardened gaze with her outwardly composed one even as her stomach nosedived at the extraordinary step she was taking. 'I want two hundred and fifty thousand pounds.'

His brows lifted a fraction but, apart from that, his expression gave nothing away. 'I'll see that you get it within the next hour or two.'

'So—' she hastily disguised a tight little swallow '—it's not…too much?'

He brought her up against the trajectory of his arousal, the shock of the contact sending a wave of heat like a furnace blast right through her body. 'I'll let you know,' he said and sealed her mouth with the blistering heat of his.

CHAPTER NINE

WHEN ELIZA WOKE the following morning her body tingled from head to foot. She turned her head but the only sign of Leo having shared the bed with her was the indentation on his pillow beside her.

And his smell…

She breathed in the musk and citrusy scent of him that clung to the sheets as well as her skin. His love-making last night had been as spine-tingling as ever, maybe even more so. For some reason the fact that he was paying her to sleep with him had made her stretch her boundaries with him. It had been heart-stopping and exciting, edgy and wonderfully, mind-blowingly satisfying.

The door of the bedroom opened and he came in carrying a cup of tea and toast on a tray. He was naked except for a pair of track pants that were slung low on his lean hips. 'I've already checked on Alessandra. Marella's giving her breakfast downstairs.'

'I'm sorry…' Eliza frowned as she pulled the sheet up to cover her naked breasts. 'I overslept…I didn't hear her on the monitor.'

'It didn't go off.' He put the tray down on her side of the bed. 'I took it with me. She woke up while I was down making the tea.'

She pushed a matted tangle of hair off her face with a sweep of her hand. This cosy little domestic scene was not what she was expecting from him. It caught her off guard. It made her feel as if she was acting in a play but she had been given the wrong script. She didn't know what was expected of her. 'You seem to be having some problems with your human resources department,' she commented dryly.

His dark glinting eyes met hers as he sat on the edge of the bed beside her. 'How so?'

She gave him an ironic look. 'Your housekeeper is acting as the nanny and your nanny is acting like the lady of the manor—or should I say lady of the villa?'

He trailed the tip of his index finger down the length of her bare arm in a lazy, barely touching stroke that set off a shower of sparks beneath her skin. 'Marella enjoys helping with Alessandra. And I quite enjoy having you playing lady of the villa.'

Eliza shivered as that bottomless dark gaze smouldered as it held hers. 'Wouldn't lady of the night be more appropriate?' she asked with a pert hitch of her chin.

A line of steel travelled from his mouth and lodged itself in his eyes. 'What do you want the money for?'

She gave a careless shrug and shifted her gaze to the left of his. 'The usual things—clothes, jewellery, shoes, salon treatments, a holiday or two.'

He captured her chin and made her look at him. 'You do realise I would have paid you much more?'

Her stomach quivered as his thumb grazed the fullness of her bottom lip. 'Yes…I know.'

He measured her gaze with his for endless, heart-chugging seconds. 'But you didn't ask for it.'

'No.'

'Why not?'

She gave another careless little shrug. 'Maybe I don't think I'm worth it.'

His thumb caressed her cheek as he cupped her face in his hand, his gaze still rock-steady on hers. 'Why would you think that?'

Eliza felt the danger of getting too close to him, of allowing him to see behind the paper-thin armour she had pinned around herself. She had to stay streetwise and smart-mouthed. She couldn't allow him to see any other version of herself.

The real version.

'You get what you pay for in life, wouldn't you agree?' She didn't pause for him to answer. 'Say my price was a million pounds. I figure this way you only got a quarter of me.'

His gaze continued to hold hers unwaveringly. 'What if I wanted all of you?'

Eliza felt a momentary flare of alarm in her chest. She had experienced his ruthless intent before. It was dangerous to be inciting it into action again. What he wanted he got. He wouldn't let anything or anyone stand in his way. Hadn't he already achieved what he'd set out to achieve? She was back in his bed, wasn't she? And it didn't look as if he was going to let her out of it any time soon. She held his look with a steady determination she wasn't even close to feeling. 'The rest of me is not for sale.'

His thumb moved back and forth over her cheek, slowly, mesmerizingly, that all-seeing, all-knowing gaze stripping away the layers of her defences like pages being torn from a cheap notepad. 'So which part have I bought?' he asked.

'The part you wanted.'

'How do you know which part I wanted?'

'It's obvious, isn't it?' She brazenly stroked a hand down his naked chest to the elastic waistband of his track pants, giving him her best sultry look. 'It's the same part I want of you.'

She heard him suck in a breath as her hand dipped below the fabric. She felt his abdomen tense. She felt the satin of his skin, the hot, hard heat of him scorching her fingers as they wrapped around him. Her body primed itself for his possession and she didn't care how sweet or savage it was going to be.

She yanked his track pants down further and bent her head to him, teasing him mercilessly with her tongue. He groaned and dug his fingers into her scalp but he didn't pull away, or, at least, not at first. She drew on him, tasting the essence of him, swirling her tongue over and around him, making little flicking movements and little cat-like licks until finally he could stand no more.

'Wait,' he gasped, trying to pull back. 'I'm going to—' He let out a short, sharp expletive as she went for broke. She had him by the hips and dug her fingers in hard. Her mouth sucked harder and harder, wanting his final capitulation the same way he went for hers—ruthlessly.

He came explosively but she didn't shy away from receiving him. He shuddered and quaked, finally sagging over her like a puppet whose strings had been suddenly severed.

Eliza caressed her hands over his back and shoulders, a slow exploratory massage of each of his carved and toned muscles. He had loved her massaging him in the past. And she had loved doing it. He had carried a lot of tension in his body even back then. There was something almost worshipful about touching him this way, with long and smooth strokes of her palms and fingers, rediscovering him like a precious memory she thought she had lost for ever. 'You've got knots in your shoulders. You need to relax more.'

'Can't get more relaxed than this right now.'

'I'm just saying…'

He lifted himself up on his elbows and locked gazes with her. 'We're doing this the wrong way around. It's not the way I usually do things.'

She tiptoed her fingers over his pectoral muscles. 'You're paying me to pleasure you. That changes the dynamic, surely?'

He pulled her hand away from his chest and sat upright, his expression contorted with a brooding frown, his gaze dark and disapproving. 'I know what you're doing.'

'What am I doing?'

'You're playing the hooker card.'

She gave a little up and down movement of one shoulder. 'If the shoe fits I usually wear it. I find it's more comfortable that way.'

'Is that really how you want to play things?'

Her brow arched haughtily. 'Do I have a choice?'

He held her gaze for a long pause before he let out a breath and got to his feet. He scraped a hand through his hair before he dropped it back down by his side. 'The money is in your account. I deposited it an hour ago.'

'Thank you.' She gave him a look. 'Sir.'

There was another tight pause before he spoke. 'I have to go to Paris on business. Marella has agreed to be here to help you with Alessandra. I don't expect you to be on duty twenty-four hours a day.'

'How long will you be away?'

'A day or two.'

'Why don't you take us with you?' she asked. 'It's a shortish trip. It shouldn't be too hard to organise. It would be a little adventure for Alessandra. It will build her confidence to travel and mix with other people other than just you and Marella and me.'

His jaw tightened like a clamp. 'Maybe some other time.'

Eliza suspected his 'maybe some other time' meant *no* other time. What did he think was going to happen to Alessandra if she stepped outside the villa for once? How was his little girl supposed to live a normal life if he kept her away from everything that was normal? 'You can't keep her hidden away for ever, you know.'

'Is that what you think I'm doing?'

'No one even knows you have a child, much less that she's blind.'

'I don't want my daughter to be ridiculed or pitied in the press.' His gaze nailed hers. 'Can you imagine how terrifying it would be for her to be hounded by paparazzi? She's too young to cope with all of that. I won't allow her to be treated like a freak show every time she goes out in public.'

'I understand how you feel, but she needs to—'

He stabbed a finger in the air towards her, his eyes blazing with vitriolic anger. 'You do *not* understand. You don't have any idea of what it's like to have a child with a disability. She can't *see.* Do you hear me? She can't see and there's not a damn thing I can do about it.'

Eliza swallowed unevenly, her heart contracting at the raw emotion he was displaying. He was angry and bitter but beneath all that was a loving father who was truly heartbroken that he could do nothing to help his little daughter. Tears burned in the back of her throat for what he was going through. No wonder he was always so tense and on edge. 'I'm sorry…'

He drew in a tight breath and released it in a slow, uneven stream. 'I'm sorry for shouting at you.'

'You don't have to apologise…'

He came back to where she was still sitting amongst the pillows, a rueful look on his face as he brushed a flyaway strand of her hair off her face. 'I know you're only trying to help but this is a lot for me to handle right now.'

She lowered her gaze again and bit at her lip. 'I shouldn't have said anything…'

He stroked the pad of his thumb over her savaged lip. 'Of course you should. You're an expert on handling children. I appreciate your opinion although I might not always agree with it.'

'I just thought it would be good for Alessandra to stretch her wings a bit.' She met his gaze again. 'But the press thing is difficult. I can see why you want to protect her from all of that. But sooner or later she'll have to deal with it. She can't stay here at the villa for the rest of her life. She needs to mix with other children, to make friends and do normal kid stuff like go to birthday parties and on picnics and play dates.'

He studied her features for a measured pause. 'I might have to go back to London some time next week. If you think Alessandra would cope with it then maybe we could make a little holiday out of it. Maybe take her to Kew Gardens or something. Smell a few roses. That sort of thing.'

Eliza gave him a soft smile and touched his hand where it was resting on the bed beside her. 'She's a very lucky little girl to have such a wonderful father like you. There are a lot of little girls out there who would give anything to be loved by their fathers the way you love her.'

His fingers ensnared hers, holding them in the warmth of his hand. 'You've never told me anything about your father. I remember you told me when we first met that your mother died when you were young. Is he still alive?'

She shifted her gaze to their joined hands. 'Yes, but I've only met him the once.'

'You don't get on?'

'We haven't got anything in common.' She traced a fingertip over the backs of his knuckles rather than meet his gaze. 'We live in different worlds, so to speak.'

He brought her hand up to his mouth and kissed her bent fingers, his eyes holding hers in a sensual tether that sent a wave of longing through her body. 'Your tea and toast are cold. Do you want me to get you some more?'

'You don't have to. I'm not used to being served breakfast in bed.'

He took her currently bare ring finger between his thumb and index finger, his eyes still meshed with hers. 'Doesn't your fiancé treat you like a princess?'

Eliza couldn't hold his gaze. 'Not any more.'

A silence dragged on for several moments.

'Why do you stay with him?'

'I'd rather not talk about it.'

He pushed up her chin to lock her gaze with his. 'Has he got some sort of hold over you? Are you frightened of him?'

'No, I'm not frightened of him. He's not that sort of person.'

'What sort of person is he?'

She flashed him an irritated look. 'Can we just drop

this conversation? I'm not comfortable about talking about him while I'm being paid to be in your bed.'

'Then maybe I should make sure I get my money's worth while you're here, *sì*?' He pinned her wrists either side of her head, his eyes hot and smouldering as his hard aroused body pressed her down on the mattress.

Even if her hands were free, Eliza knew she wouldn't have had the strength of will to push him away. Her lower body was on fire, aching with the need to feel him inside her. He released one of her hands so he could rip away the sheet that was covering her, his hungry gaze moving over her like a burning flame.

His mouth swooped down and covered hers in a searing kiss, his tongue driving through to meet hers in a crazy, lustful, frenzied dance. Her breasts swelled beneath the solid press of his chest, her nipples going to hard little peaks as they rubbed against him.

He reached across her to find a condom in the bedside cabinet drawer but he didn't take his mouth off hers to do it. He kissed her relentlessly, passionately, drawing from her the sort of shamelessly wanton response she'd only ever experienced with him. She used her teeth like a female tiger in heat, biting and nipping and tugging at his lower lip, teasing him with little flicks of her tongue against his, shivering in delight when he did the same back to her.

Once the condom was on he entered her with a thick, surging thrust that made her gasp out loud. There was nothing slow and languid about his lovemaking. It was a breathtakingly fast and furious ride to the summit of pleasure. She felt the pressure building so quickly it was like a pressure cooker about to explode. Her body needed only the slightest bit of extra encouragement from his fingers to send her over the edge into a tumultuous release that made her head spin along with her senses.

But he wasn't stopping things there.

Before she had even caught her breath he flipped her over on her stomach, straddling her from behind, those strong hands of his on her hips as he thrust deep and hard, again and again until she was shivering with pleasure both inside and out.

There was something so wickedly primal and earthy about this dominant position. She felt as if he was taming her, subduing her even as he pleasured her. She heard his breathing rate increase as he fought for control, the grip on her hips almost painful as he thrust above her.

She raised her bottom just a fraction and the change of friction set off an explosion of feeling that shuddered through her like an earthquake: tremor after tremor, aftershock after aftershock, until finally she came out the other side, totally spent and limbless.

His hands tightened on her hips to hold her steady as he came. She felt every spasm of his body. She heard those harsh, utterly male groans of ecstasy that delighted her so much.

Did he experience the same rush of pleasure with the other women he slept with? Was it foolish of her to think she was somehow special? That what he experienced with her was completely different than with anyone else? That the sensational heat of their physical connection was the real reason he had brought her back into his life, not just as a fill-in nanny for his daughter?

Leo turned her back over and looked at her for a long moment. It wasn't easy to read his expression. Was he, like her, trying to disguise how deeply affected he was by what they had both shared? 'I want you to promise me something.'

Eliza moistened her kiss-swollen lips. 'What?'

'If we go to London next week, there is to be no physical contact with your fiancé.'

His sudden change in mood was jarring to say the least. But then, what had she been expecting him to say?

'What are you going to do?' she asked. 'Keep me under lock and key?'

A flinty element entered his gaze as it held hers. 'I am not having you go from my bed to his and back again. Do I make myself clear?'

She resented him thinking she would do such a thing, even though she knew it was perverse of her to blame him given she hadn't told him the truth about her situation. She wondered if she should just tell him. Maybe he would understand her painful dilemma much more than she gave him credit for. Sure, she'd left it a bit late, but she might be able to make him understand how terribly conflicted she felt.

'Leo…there's something you need to know about Ewan—'

'I don't even want you to speak his name in my presence,' he said. 'I will not share you with him or anyone. I've paid for your time and I will not be short-changed or cuckolded.' He got off the bed and picked up his track pants and roughly pulled them back up over his hips.

Her pride finally came to her rescue. She swung her legs off the bed and, with scant regard for her nakedness, stalked over to where he was standing and poked her index finger into the middle of his chest like a probe. 'How dare you tell me who I can and can't speak about in your presence?' she said. 'I don't care how much money you pay me. I will *not* be ordered about by you.'

His eyes glittered as he stared her down. 'You will do as I say or suffer the consequences.'

She curled her lip at him. 'Is that supposed to scare me? Because, if so, it doesn't.' *It did, but she wasn't going to admit that.*

His mouth was a thin line of ruthless determination. 'You want a job to go back to at the end of the summer break? Then think very carefully about your behaviour. One word from me and your career as a teacher will be well and truly over.'

Outrage made her splutter. 'You can't do that!'

His hardened look said he could and he would. 'I'll see you when I get back.'

CHAPTER TEN

IT WAS ALMOST a week before Eliza saw Leo again. Apparently the project he had in Paris had developed some issues and he needed to be on site to handle the difficulties. She had no doubt his work was demanding and time consuming, but in this instance she wondered if he had deliberately taken himself out of the picture to regroup. He didn't speak to her for long each time he called—just long enough for her to give him updates on what Alessandra was doing. The conversations were stiff and formal, just like a powerful employer to a very low-ranked employee. It riled her deeply, but she was nearly always with Alessandra when he called so she had no recourse. She had considered calling him when Alessandra was in bed asleep but had always talked herself out of it out of stubborn and wilful pride.

Alessandra clearly missed her father being around, but she seemed to accept he had to go away to work from time to time. Eliza enjoyed being with the little girl, even though at times it was challenging to think of ways to help her become more independent. Some days Alessandra was more motivated than others. But it was lovely to have the one on one time with her after coming from a busy classroom where she had to juggle so many children's educational and social needs.

Tatiana, the orientation and mobility teacher, came for another session and was thrilled to see how Alessandra had improved over the week. To Eliza it had seemed such painfully slow progress, but Tatiana reassured her that Alessandra was doing far better than other vision-impaired children her age.

The one challenge that Eliza was particularly keen to attempt was taking Alessandra for a walk outside the villa or even down to one of the cafés in Positano. She had spoken to Marella about it in passing, but while the housekeeper thought it was a great idea, she had reservations over what Leo would say.

'Why don't you ask him about it when he next calls?' Marella said.

Eliza knew what he would say. *No.* She wanted to present it as a fait accompli to show him how well his little girl was coping with new experiences. She took comfort in the fact that no one would know who she was so there would be no threat of press attention.

Their first walk outside the villa grounds was slow, but Eliza took comfort in the fact that Alessandra seemed to enjoy the different smells and sounds the further they went. She couldn't help feeling incredibly sad as she looked down at the exquisite beauty of the scenery below. The bluey-green water of the ocean sparkled in the sunshine, boats, frightfully expensive-looking yachts and other pleasure craft dotted the surface, but Alessandra could see none of it. It seemed so cruel to be robbed of such pleasure in looking at the glorious array of nature. But then, if Alessandra had never seen it, would she miss it the way a sighted person would if their vision was suddenly taken away?

Their second outing was a little more adventurous. Eliza got Giuseppe to drive them down to Spiaggia

Fornillo, the less crowded of the two main beaches in Positano. It had been quite an achievement getting the little girl to walk on the pebbly shore with bare feet but she seemed to enjoy the experience.

'Have you ever been swimming?' Eliza asked Alessandra as they made their way back to the villa in the car.

'Kathleen took me once but I didn't like it.'

'I didn't like swimming at first either,' Eliza said, giving the little girl's hand a gentle squeeze. 'But after you get over the fear part and learn to float it's one of the nicest things to do, especially on a hot day.'

That very afternoon Eliza took Alessandra down to the pool in the garden for a swimming lesson. With plenty of sunscreen to protect the little girl's pale skin, she gently introduced her to the feel of the water by getting her to kick her legs while she held her, gradually working up to getting used to having water trickle over her face. Alessandra was frightened at first, but gradually became confident enough to float on her back with Eliza keeping her supported by a gentle hand beneath her shoulder blades and in the dish of her little back.

'Am I swimming yet?' Alessandra asked, almost swallowing a mouthful of water in her excitement.

'Almost, sweetie.' Eliza gave a little laugh. 'You're getting better all the time. Now let's try floating on your tummy. You'll have to hold your breath for this. Remember how I got you to blow bubbles into the water before?'

'Uh huh.' Alessandra turned on her stomach with Eliza's guiding hands and gingerly put her face in the water. She blew some bubbles but soon had to lift her head to snatch in a breath. She gave a few little splutters but didn't seem too fazed by the experience.

'Well done,' Eliza said. 'You're a right little water baby, aren't you?'

Alessandra grinned as she clung to Eliza like a little frog on a tree. 'I like swimming now. And I like you. I wish you could stay with me for ever.'

Eliza's heart contracted sharply at the unexpected love she felt for this little child. 'I like you too, darling.' *And I wish I could stay for ever too.*

A tall shadow suddenly blocked the angle of the sun and she turned and saw Leo standing there with an unreadable expression on his face. 'Oh…I didn't realise you were back…Alessandra, your father is home.'

'*Papà*, I can swim!'

'I saw you, *mia piccola*,' Leo said, leaning down to kiss her on both cheeks. 'I'm very impressed. Is there room in there for me?'

'Yes!'

Eliza didn't say a word. She wasn't sure it was wise to share the pool—even as big as it was—with that tall, intensely male, leanly muscled body. Wearing a bikini when accompanied by a blind toddler was quite different from wearing it when there was a fully sighted, full-blooded man around, especially one who had seen her in much less. She felt the scorch of his gaze as it went to the curve of her breasts, which were showing just above the line of the water she was standing in. She felt her insides clench and release with that intimate tug of need she only felt when he was around.

A silent message passed between their locked gazes.

Eliza gulped as he stood back up and tugged at his tie, pulling it through the collar of his shirt to toss it to one of the sun loungers on the sandstone terrace beside the pool.

His shirt was next, followed by his shoes and socks.

The sun caught the angles and planes of his taut chest and abdomen, making him look like a statue carved by a master of the art.

Marella came out on to the terrace at that point with a tray of iced drinks. 'I think it might be time for Alessandra to get out of the heat, *sì*?' she said with a twinkling and rather knowing smile.

Eliza felt a blush rush over her face and travel to the very roots of her hair. 'It's my job to see to her—'

'*Grazie,* Marella,' Leo said smoothly. 'I think Eliza could do with some time to relax.' He bent and scooped Alessandra out of her arms. 'I will be up later to tuck you into bed, *tesorina*. Be good for Marella.'

Once Marella and the child had gone Eliza was left feeling alarmingly defenceless. She covered her chest with her arms, shivering even though the sun was still deliciously warm on her neck and shoulders. 'What are you doing?' she asked.

His hands were pulling his belt through the lugs of his trousers. 'I'm joining you in the pool.'

'But you're not wearing bathers…are you?'

A dark brow lifted in an arc. 'I seem to remember a time when you didn't think they were necessary.'

'That was before. It was different then. This place is like Piccadilly Circus. There are staff about everywhere.'

He unzipped his trousers and she watched with bated breath as he stood there in nothing but his black underwear. He already had the beginnings of an erection, which was no surprise given how her own body was reacting. 'Have you missed me, *cara*?'

She gave her head a haughty little toss. 'No.'

He laughed and slipped into the water beside her, cupping the back of her head with one of his hands as he pressed a hot kiss to her tight mouth. It didn't stay tight for long, however. All it took was one erotic sweep of his tongue for her to open to him with a sigh of bliss. He tasted salty and male with a hint of mint. It was ambrosia to her. She responded greedily, giving back as good as he gave, her tongue tangling, duelling and seducing just as his was doing to hers. Her breasts were jammed up against his chest, the water-soaked fabric abrading her already erect nipples.

His other hand ruthlessly undid the strings of her bikini top and it floated away from her body like a four-legged octopus. He cupped her free breasts with his hands, caressing her, teasing her with his warm, wet touch. He took his mouth off hers to feast on each breast in turn. Eliza arched back in pleasure as his teeth and his tongue grazed and salved in turn. Her nerves went into a sensual riot beneath her skin. They jumped and danced and flickered with longing. That deepest, most feminine ache of all pulsed relentlessly between her legs. She could feel his hard erection pressing against the softness of her belly. It awoke everything that was female in her. She rubbed against him to get more of that wonderful friction.

He made a guttural sound in his throat as he undid the strings of her bikini bottoms at her hips. The scanty fabric fell away and his fingers went to her, delving deep.

It wasn't enough. She wanted more. She wanted *all* of him.

She pulled at his underwear to free him to her touch. She wrapped her hand around him, rubbing him, teasing him, and pleasuring him as his mouth came back to hers in a passionately hot kiss that had undercurrents of desperation.

He suddenly pulled back from her, breathing hard, his eyes glazed with desire. 'I haven't got a condom.'

'Oh…' Disappointment was like an enervating drug that made her sag as if all of her muscles were weighted by anvils.

His eyes gleamed at her as he backed her against the side of the pool. 'Why the long face, *tesoro mio*? We can be creative, *sì*?'

Her body tingled at the thought of just how creative his lovemaking could be. But then, she too could be innovative when it came to giving him pleasure. She slithered against him, from chest to thigh, ramping up his need for her with the same merciless intent he had been using on her.

He took her by the waist and lifted her up to a sitting position on the edge of the pool. It was shamelessly wanton to open her legs in full view of the villa but she was beyond caring.

The first stroke of his masterful tongue made her shudder, the second made her gasp, and the third made her cry out loud as the ripples started to roll through her. 'Don't stop, don't stop, *don't stop…*' She clung to his hair for purchase as her body shattered around her.

He gave her a sexy smile as she came back to her senses. 'Good?'

She gave a little shrug that belied everything she had just felt. 'OK, I guess.'

'Minx.' He pulled her back into the water to hold her against him. 'I should punish you for lying. What do you think would be a suitable penance?'

Send me back to my old life. Eliza gave herself a mental shake and forced a smile to her lips. 'I don't know…I'm sure you'll think of something.'

His brows moved together. 'What's wrong?'

'Nothing.'

He cupped her cheek, holding her gaze with his. 'Are you still angry with me?'

Eliza was starting to wonder where her anger had gone. As soon as he had appeared on the pool deck she had forgotten all about their tense little battle of wills the day he had left to go to Paris. Her feelings about him now were much more confusing…terrifying, actually. She couldn't afford to examine them too closely.

'Does it matter to you what I feel?' she asked. 'I'm just an employee. I'm not supposed to feel anything but gratitude for having a job.'

His expression became brooding as his hand dropped away from her face. 'So we're back to that, are we?'

'You're the one who engineered this,' she said, struggling to keep her emotions in check. 'You come marching back in my life and issue orders and stipulations and conditions. I don't know what you want from me. You keep changing the goalposts. I just don't know who I'm supposed to be when I'm with you.'

He looked at her for a lengthy moment. 'Why not just be yourself?'

She gave a little cough of despair. 'I don't even know who that is any more.'

His hands came down on the tops of her shoulders, a gentle but firm hold. His eyes were very dark as they meshed with hers, but not with anger this time. 'Who was that girl in the bar four years ago?'

Eliza twisted her lips in a rueful manner. 'I'm not sure. I hadn't met her before that night. She came as a bit of a surprise to me, to be perfectly honest.'

He started massaging his thumbs over the front of her shoulders, slowly and soothingly. 'She came as a bit of a surprise to me, too. A delightful one, however.'

She felt a wave of sadness wash over her. How very different things would have been if she had been free to commit to the relationship he had wanted. 'Did you really fall in love with me back then?' She was shocked she had asked it but it was too late to take the words back. They hung in the silence for a beat or two.

'I think you were right when you said I was looking for stability after my father died. Losing him so suddenly threw me. I think it's hard for an only child—no matter how young or old—to deal with the loss of a parent. There's no one to share the grief with. I panicked at the thought of ending up like him, all alone and desperately lonely.'

'I'm sorry.'

He gave her shoulders a little squeeze before he dropped his hands. 'You'd better get some clothes on. You're starting to get goose bumps.'

Eliza watched as he effortlessly hauled himself out of the pool. He was completely unselfconscious about being naked. He stepped into his trousers and zipped them up without even bothering to dry himself. He bent to pick up his shoes and, flinging his shirt and tie over one shoulder, walked into the villa without a backward glance.

When Eliza came down to the *salone* later that evening Leo was standing with his back to the room with a drink in his hand. There was something about his posture that suggested he was no longer in that mellow mood he'd been in down by the pool. He turned as she came in and gave her a brittle glare. 'Alessandra informed me you'd taken her outside the villa grounds on not one, but two occasions.'

She straightened her shoulders. 'We didn't go very far. She'd never been to the beach before.'

'That's completely beside the point.' His eyes blazed with anger. 'Do you have any idea of the risk you were taking?'

'What risk is there in allowing her to walk down the street or put her feet in the ocean, for God's sake? I was with her the whole time.'

'You went expressly against my instructions.'

Eliza frowned at him. 'But you said we'd go to London next week. I thought it would be good preparation for that.'

'I said I'd *think* about it.'

'That's not the way I heard it. You said if I thought Alessandra would cope with it then we'd make a little holiday out of it. I was preparing her to cope with it and she did very well, all things considered.'

Anger pulsed at the side of his mouth. 'Did anyone see you? Were there paparazzi about?'

'No, why should there be?' she asked. 'No one knows who I am.'

'That could change as soon as we are seen in public together.' His eyes pinned hers. 'Have you thought of how you're going to explain *that* to your fiancé?'

Eliza raised her chin defiantly. 'Yes, I have thought about it. I'll tell him the truth.'

His brow furrowed. 'That I'm paying you to sleep with me?'

She gave him an arch look. 'It's the truth, isn't it?'

He shifted his gaze and let out a gust of a breath. 'It wasn't why I asked you to come here.'

'So you keep saying, but it's pretty obvious this is what you wanted right from the start.'

He took a large swallow of his drink and put it down,

his muscles bunched and tight beneath the fine cotton of his shirt. 'You haven't forgotten you're forbidden to speak to the press, have you?'

'No.'

He faced her with a steely look. 'You're not very good at obeying rules, are you, Eliza?'

'You're very good at making them up as you go along, aren't you?' she tossed back.

His mouth started to twitch at the corners. 'I wondered when she would be back.'

She frowned again. 'What...*who* do you mean?'

'The girl in the bar—that spirited, feisty, edgy little temptress.' His eyes glinted darkly. 'I like her. She turns me on.'

She made a huffy movement with one of her shoulders, trying to ignore the wave of heat that was coursing through her at that smouldering look in his gaze. 'Yes, well, I liked the guy by the pool this afternoon much more than the one facing me now.'

'What did you like about him?'

'He was nice.'

'Nice?' He gave a laugh. 'That's not a word I would ever use to describe myself.'

'You were nice four years ago. I thought you were one of the nicest men I'd ever met.'

His dark eyes gleamed some more. 'Even though I practically ripped the clothes from your body and had wild, rough sex with you the first night we met?'

'Did I complain?'

'No.' His frown came back and the ghost of a smile that had been playing about his mouth disappeared. 'Why did you come up to my room with me that night?'

'I told you—I was tipsy and jet-lagged and feeling reckless.'

'You were taking a hell of a risk. I could have been anyone. I could have hurt you—seriously hurt you.'

'I trusted you.'

'Foolish, foolish girl.'

Eliza felt a shiver run up along her arms. She could see the desire he had for her. She could feel it pulsing like a current in the air between them. 'The way I see it, you were taking a similar risk.'

The ghost of a smile was back, wry this time as it tilted up one corner of his mouth. 'I find it hard to see what you could have possibly done to hurt me. I'm almost twice your weight.'

But I did hurt you, she thought. *Isn't that why I'm here now?*

'Are you going to pour me a drink or do I have to jump through hoops first?' she asked.

'No hoops.' He came to stand right in front of her. 'Just one kiss.'

She tilted her head back and held his dark brown gaze pertly as the blood all but sizzled in her veins. 'Is that an order?'

He tugged her against his rock-hard body, his eyes scorching hers. 'You bet it is.'

CHAPTER ELEVEN

WHEN ELIZA BROUGHT Alessandra downstairs for breakfast the next morning Leo intercepted them at the door. He reached for his daughter and held her close against his broad chest. Seeing such an intensely masculine man hold a tiny child so protectively made Eliza's heart instantly melt.

Was it her imagination that he seemed a little more relaxed this morning? It wasn't as if he was particularly rested, but then, neither was she. Their lovemaking last night had been particularly passionate and edgy. She could still feel the little pull of tender muscles where he had thrust so deep and so hard inside her. It was such a heady reminder of the breathtaking mastery he had over her body. But as much as she loved the heart-stopping raciness of his lovemaking, there was a tiny part of her that secretly longed for something a little more emotional. Maybe he didn't have the capacity to feel emotion during sex. It was just a physical release for him, like any other bodily need being attended to, like hunger and thirst. But it wasn't like that for her… or at least not now…

'I thought we could have breakfast out on the water this morning,' Leo said. 'Would you like that, *mia piccola*?'

'In the pool?' Alessandra asked.

'No, on my boat.'

'You have a boat?' Eliza asked.

'It's moored down at the marina. I thought Alessandra might enjoy being out on the water. I've never taken her on it before. Marella's packing us up a picnic to take with us.'

Eliza could see he was making an effort to spend more time with his daughter. He was relaxing his tight control over where she could go. She could also see what a big step it was for him to take. A trip out on a boat might be a relatively simple and rather enjoyable adventure for a sighted child, but in Alessandra's case there were many considerations to take into account. Her experience of the outing would be different but hopefully no less enjoyable. Besides, she would be with her father and that was clearly something that made her feel loved and special.

'Breakfast on the water sounds lovely, doesn't it, sweetie?' she addressed the little girl.

Alessandra hugged her arms tightly around her father's neck and smiled. 'Can I take Rosie with me?'

'Who's Rosie?' Leo asked.

'Rosie is the toy puppy Eliza made for me,' Alessandra said. 'She has long floppy ears and a tail just like a real puppy.'

Leo met Eliza's gaze over the top of his daughter's little head. 'Eliza is a very clever young lady. She is talented at many things.'

'I want her to stay with me for ever,' Alessandra said. 'Can you make her stay with us, *Papà*? I want her to be my *mamma* now. She tucks me in and reads me stories and she cuddles me lots and lots.'

Eliza felt emotion block her throat like a scrubbing brush stuck halfway down. She blinked a couple of times and shifted her gaze from Leo's. Alessandra needed someone there *all* of the time, someone she could rely on—someone to love her unconditionally.

Hadn't *she* felt the same desperate ache for stability and love as a child? Throughout her lonely childhood she had clutched on to various caregivers in an attempt to feel loved and cherished. Whenever she had been sent to yet another foster placement, she had blamed herself for not being pretty enough, cute enough or lovable enough. The constant pressure of wondering whether she was doing the right thing to make people love her had worn her down. She had eventually stopped trying and at times had deliberately sabotaged the relationships that could have most helped her.

But Alessandra wasn't a difficult child to love. Eliza loved all children—even the most trying ones—but something about Leo's little girl had planted a tiny fish-hook in her heart. She felt it tugging on her whenever she thought of the day when her time with her would come to an end. Leaving Leo would break her heart, leaving his daughter would rip it from her chest.

'I'm afraid that's not possible,' Leo said in a matter-of-fact tone. 'Now, let's go and get that picnic, shall we?'

Leo's motor launch was moored amongst similar luxury boats down at the marina. It was a beautiful vessel, sleek and powerful as it carved through the water. The sun was bright and made thousands of diamonds sparkle across the surface of the sea. It was a poignant reminder that little Alessandra couldn't see the beauty that surrounded them. But she was clearly enjoying being in the fresh air with the briny scent of the sea in the air. She lifted her face to the breeze as the boat moved across the water and giggled in delight when a spray of moisture hit her face. 'It's wetting me!'

'The ocean is blowing you kisses,' Eliza said and dropped a kiss on the top of the little girl's wind-tousled hair. She looked up and caught Leo's gaze on her. 'It's a gorgeous boat, Leo. Have you had it long?'

'I bought it just before Alessandra was born.' He brushed back his hair off his face with one of his hands, and although he was wearing reflective sunglasses she could see the crease of a frown between his brows. 'I thought it'd be a great thing to do as a family. Get out on the water, sail into the sunset, get away from the madding crowd, so to speak.' His mouth twisted ruefully. 'I only ever take it out on my own, mostly late at night when Alessandra's fast asleep in bed when Kathleen or Marella are on duty. I suppose I should think about selling it.'

Eliza looked at his wind-tousled hair and her heart gave a little leap of hope. 'Is that where you went the other night? Out here on the boat…alone?'

His expression was self-deprecating. 'Not quite what you were expecting from a worldly playboy, is it?'

Eliza was conscious of Alessandra sitting on her knee but she hoped the unfamiliar English words would not compromise her innocence. 'When was the last time you were…um…a playboy?'

'I took my marriage vows seriously, even though nothing was happening in that department, more or less since that first night. We agreed to leave things on a platonic basis. In the time since she…left us ten months ago…' he glanced at his daughter for a moment before returning his gaze to hers '…I've had other more important priorities.'

Eliza stared at him in shock. For the last four years

he had not been out with a variety of mistresses. He hadn't been with *anyone.* Like her, he had been concentrating on his responsibilities, trying to do the best he could under difficult and heart-wrenching circumstances. The night she had thought he had been having bed-wrecking sex with some casual hook-up, he had actually been out on his boat—*alone.* Probably spending the time like she did back in her life in England, tortured with guilt and desperation at how life had thrown such a devastating curve ball.

Alessandra shifted on Eliza's lap. 'I'm hungry.'

Eliza ruffled the little tot's raven-black hair. 'Then let's have breakfast.'

Leo met her gaze and gave her a smile. 'How about you set up the picnic in the dining area while I teach this young lady how to steer a motor launch?'

'Can I steer it? Can I really?' Alessandra asked with excitement. 'What if I run into something?'

He scooped her up in his arms and carried her towards the bow. 'You'll have me by your side to direct you, *mia piccola.* We'll be a team. A team works together so no one gets into trouble. We look out for each other.'

'Can Eliza be part of our team?' Alessandra asked. 'For always and always?'

Eliza blinked back a rush of tears and looked out at the ocean so Leo couldn't see how much his little girl's request had pained her. Why was life always so full of such difficult choices? If she chose to stay she would be abandoning Samantha and Ewan. If she chose to leave she would be breaking not only her own heart, but also dear little Alessandra's.

As for Leo's heart…did he still have one after what happened between them four years ago? She had a feeling he had closed off his heart since then. Yes, he loved his daughter, but he would allow no one else to get close to him.

'She's a part of our team for now,' he said in a deep and gravelly tone. 'Now, let's get your hands on the wheel. Yes, just like that. Now, here we go—full steam ahead.'

On the way back to the marina after breakfast, Leo glanced at Eliza, who was sitting with his daughter on her lap, holding one of her little hands in hers with an indulgent smile on her face. To anyone looking from the outside, she would easily pass for Alessandra's biological mother with her glossy mahogany hair and creamy toned skin.

Although he had paid an enormous sum of money to engage her services as a nanny, he suspected she would have been just as dedicated if he had paid her nothing. She seemed to genuinely care for his daughter. He had seen her numerous times when she hadn't known he was watching. Those spontaneous hugs and kisses she gave Alessandra could not be anything but genuine.

Even his housekeeper, Marella, had commented on how much happier Alessandra seemed now that Eliza was there. Truth be told, he had found it a little unnerving to see Eliza's relationship grow and blossom with his daughter. He hadn't planned on Alessandra getting so attached to her so quickly. He had felt confident Alessandra's relationship with Kathleen would override any new feelings she developed for Eliza.

And, as much as he hated to admit it, the villa did seem more of a home with the sound of laughter and footsteps going up and down the corridors. Eliza had enhanced his daughter's life in such a short time. Her swimming lessons and her trips to the beach had built his daughter's awareness of the world around her. Eliza's competence and confidence in exposing Alessandra to new things had helped give him the confidence to take this outing today. She had shown him that he could afford to be more adventurous in taking Alessandra out and about more. His little girl might not be able to see the things he so desperately wanted her to see, but she had clearly enjoyed the sunshine and the fresh air and the sound of the water and the sea birds. How much more could he help her experience?

But how could he do it without Eliza?

When they returned from the trip to London there would be less than ten days left before Kathleen returned. She had emailed him and told him she wasn't going to stay in Ireland with her family after all. A couple of weeks ago he would have been thrilled by that announcement.

But now…he wasn't sure he wanted to think about how he felt.

Eliza hadn't been wearing her engagement ring but he had noticed it swinging on a chain around her neck a couple of times. She took care never to wear it when they were in bed together but it irked him that she still clung to it. He knew she wasn't in love with the guy and yet he didn't like to fool himself that she was in love with him instead.

Their arrangement was purely a sexual one, not an emotional one. He was happy with that. Perhaps happy was not the best choice of word—content, satisfied…

OK, frustrated was probably a little closer to how he was feeling. He always felt as if she gave everything of herself physically when they were together but there was a part of her that was still off-limits.

What perverse facet of his personality craved that one elusive part of her that she refused to offer him? It wasn't as if he loved her. He had sworn he would never allow himself to be that vulnerable again. Hadn't he learnt that lesson the hard way in childhood? He had loved his mother and look how she had walked out as if he had meant nothing to her.

He flatly *refused* to let anyone do that to him again.

He had been caught off guard with Eliza four years ago. The sudden death of his father had left him reeling. He had seen something in Eliza that had spoken directly to his damaged soul. He had felt as if they were kindred spirits. He knew that it sounded like some sort of crystal ball claptrap, but it had stayed with him all the same—the sense that they had both experienced bitter disappointment in life and were searching for some way of soothing that deep ache in their psyche. Their physical connection had transcended anything he had experienced before. Even now his body was humming with the aftershocks of their lovemaking last night. No one pleasured him the way she did. He suspected no one pleasured her the way he did, either.

But she wasn't going to stay with him for ever. He wasn't going to ask her to. He would have to let her go when the time was up. He would have no need of her as a nanny now that Kathleen was coming back.

And those other needs?

Well, there were other women, weren't there? Women who wanted what he wanted: a temporary, mutually satisfying arrangement with no feelings, no attachment and no regrets once it was over.

He had lived the life of a playboy before. He could do it again.

* * *

Eliza was sitting on deck with Alessandra fast asleep against her shoulder as Leo docked the vessel when she caught sight of a photographer aiming a powerful-looking lens their way. 'Um…Leo?'

He glanced across at her. 'What's wrong?'

She jerked her head in the direction of the cameraman. 'It might be just a tourist…'

'Take Alessandra below deck,' he commanded curtly.

'I don't think—'

'Do as I say,' he clipped out.

Eliza rose stiffly to her feet and, putting a protective hand to the back of the little child's head, went back down below deck. She tucked Alessandra into one of the beds in one of the luxury sleeping suites and gently closed the door. She sat in the lounge and fumed about Leo's curt manner. She understood he wanted to protect his little daughter but the bigger the issue he made out of it the more anxious Alessandra might become. She felt it would be better to explain to Alessandra that there were journalists out and about who were interested in her Papà's life and that it was part and parcel of being a successful public figure.

And how dare he speak to *her* as if she was just a servant? They were lovers for God's sake! It might be a temporary arrangement and all that, but she refused to be spoken to as if she had no standing with him at all.

Leo came down to the lounge after a few minutes, his expression black with anger. 'When I ask you to do something I expect you to do it, not stand there arguing about it.'

Eliza got abruptly to her feet and shot him a glare. 'You didn't ask me. You *ordered* me.'

His mouth tightened until his lips all but disappeared. 'You will do as I ask or order, do you hear me?'

She glowered at him. 'I will not be spoken to like that. And what if Alessandra had been awake? What's she going to think if she hears you barking out orders as if I'm nothing to you but yet another obsequious servant you've surrounded yourself with to make your life run like stupid clockwork?'

His dark gaze took on a probing glint. 'Are you saying you want to be more to me than an employee?'

Eliza rued her reckless tongue. 'No…no, I'm not saying that.'

'Then what are you saying?'

She blew out a tense little breath. What *was* she saying? She wanted to be more to him than a temporary fling but he was never going to ask her and she wasn't free to accept if by some miracle he did. 'I'm saying you have no right to order me about like a drill sergeant. There will always be journalists lurking about. You have to prepare Alessandra for it. She's old enough to understand that people are interested in your life.'

He scraped a hand through his hair, making it even more tousled than the wind had done. 'I'm sorry. I was wrong to snap at you. It just caught me off guard seeing that guy with that camera up there.'

'Was it a journalist?'

'Probably. I'm not sure what paper or agency he works for. It doesn't seem to matter. The photos go viral within minutes.' His expression tightened. 'I can't stand the thought of my daughter being the target of intrusive paparazzi. I'm not ready to expose her to that.'

'I know this is really hard for you,' Eliza said. 'But Alessandra will feel your tension if you don't relax a bit. Other high profile parents have to deal with this stuff all the time. The more you try and resist these people, the more attractive you become as a target.'

'You're probably right…' He gave her a worn down look. 'I always swore I would never let her go through a childhood like mine. I want to protect her as much as I can. I want her to feel safe and loved.'

'What was it like during your childhood?'

He sucked in another breath and released it in a whoosh. 'It certainly wasn't all tartan picnic blankets and soft cuddly puppies. I think my mother needed to justify her decision to leave by publicly documenting a whole list of infringements my father and I had supposedly done. I was just a little kid. What had I done other than be a kid? My father…well, all he had done was love her. The press made the most of it, of course. The scandal of my mother's affair was splashed over every paper in the country but she didn't seem to care. It was as if she was proud to have got away from the shackles of domesticity. It destroyed my father. He just crumpled emotionally to think he wasn't enough for her—that she had sold out to someone who had more money than him.'

Eliza could understand now why he had such a fierce desire to keep Alessandra out of the probing eyes of the media. He had been caught in the crossfire as a child. How distressing it must have been to have all those private issues made public. She put a hand on his arm. 'You weren't to blame for your parents' problems.'

He looked down at her for a long moment, his gaze deep and dark. 'How did your mother die?'

She dropped her hand from his arm and turned away, folding her arms across her body. 'What has that got to do with anything?'

'You've never told me. I want to know. What happened to her?'

Eliza blew out a breath and faced him again. What was the point of hiding it? She was the product of despair and degradation. It couldn't be changed. She couldn't miraculously whitewash her background any more than he could his. 'Drugs and drink robbed her of her life. They robbed me of both my parents when it comes down to it. I suspect my father was the one who introduced her to drugs. He's serving time in prison for drug-related offences. The one and only time I visited him he asked me to drug run for him. It might seem strange, given that familial blood is supposed to be thicker than water, but I declined. I guess it had something to do with the fact that I was farmed out to distant relatives who weren't all that enamoured with the prospect of raising a young, bewildered and overly sensitive child. The only true family I've known is my fiancé's. So, as to tartan picnic blankets and puppies… well, I have no experience of that, either.'

He put a gentle hand on her shoulder. 'I'm sorry.'

Eliza gave him the vestige of a smile. 'Why are you apologising? It's not your fault. I was already royally screwed up when I met you.'

His eyes roved her face, lingering over her gaze as if searching for the real person hiding behind the shadows. 'Maybe, but I probably made it a whole lot worse.'

'You didn't.' She put her hand on his chest, feeling his heart beating slow and steadily underneath her palm. 'I was happy for those three weeks. It was like stepping into someone else's life. For that period of time I didn't have a care in the world. It was like a dream, a fantasy. I didn't want it to end.'

'Then why did you end it?'

Her hand slid off his chest to push through the curtain of her windswept hair. 'All good things have to come to an end, don't they? It was time to move on. Soon it will be time to move on again.'

'What about Alessandra? You've been very good for her—even Tatiana says so. And it's easy to see how attached she's become to you.'

Eliza felt that painful little fishhook tug on her heart again. 'She'll cope. She'll have Kathleen and Marella and, most importantly, she'll have you.'

'Will you miss her?'

'I'll miss her terribly. She's such a little sweetheart.' *I wish she were mine.*

'And what about me?' His eyes were suddenly unreadable. 'Will you miss me too?'

Eliza's heart gave another painful contraction at the thought of leaving him. Would their paths ever cross again? Would the only contact be seeing him from time to time in a gossip magazine with some other woman on his arm? How would she bear it? What if he *did* decide to marry again? He might go on to have another child, or even more than one. He would have the family she had longed for while she would be stuck in her bleak, lonely life back at home, trapped in an engagement with a man who could not free her from it even if he wanted to.

She forced a worldly smile to her lips. 'I'll certainly miss picnics on luxury launches and swanning about in a villa that's as big as an apartment block.'

'That wasn't what I was asking.'

'Just what exactly *are* you asking?' She gave him a pointed look. 'It's not like you want me to stay with you permanently—Kathleen is coming back. You won't need me any more.'

'We'd better get going.' His expression was a mask of stone. 'I have some work to see to before we leave for London tomorrow.'

'We're leaving *tomorrow*?'

'The bursar of your school wants to meet with me. He spoke of a project you had proposed to the board for young single mothers on parenting practices and counselling, especially for those with children with special needs. I'd like to look at it a little more closely. It sounds like a good idea.'

Eliza had trouble containing her surprise. 'I don't know what to say…'

His eyes were hard as they held hers. 'Don't go attaching anything sentimental to my interest. I have a lot of money and, like a lot of wealthy people, I want to make a difference where it counts. There are other schools and charities that are in just as much, if not more, need of funds. I have to choose the ones I think are most productive in the long run.'

'This means so much to me,' she said. 'It's been a dream of mine for so long to do something like this. I don't know how to thank you.'

'I don't want or need your thanks.' He moved to the suite where Alessandra was sleeping. 'Meet me at the car. The paparazzi guy should have left by now.'

CHAPTER TWELVE

Eliza didn't see Leo until the following morning, just as they were about to leave for London. She had waited for him last night but he hadn't come to her.

She was still so deeply touched that he was considering doing more for her school. She wasn't sure what was behind his motivation, she was just grateful that he was contemplating supporting the project that was so very dear to her heart.

Had he softened in his attitude towards her? Dare she hope that he would no longer hate her for how she had rejected him all those years ago? Was this the time to tell him about Ewan? He had expressly forbidden her to speak of her fiancé, but maybe during this trip to London she could find a quiet moment to explain to him her circumstances. He came across as such a hard-nosed businessman, but she knew he had a heart. She had seen it time and time again when he was with his tiny daughter. She caught faint glimpses of it when she found his gaze on her, as if he was studying her, trying to put things together in his head. She desperately wanted him to understand her situation. As each day passed she felt more and more that he had a right to know. She could not leave him without telling him why she had made the choice she had.

'Signor Valente wants a quick word with you in the study,' Marella said as she bundled Alessandra into her arms. 'I'll get Alessandra settled in the car. Giuseppe will take the bags.'

Eliza went through to the study, where she found Leo standing behind his desk looking out at the garden. He turned as he heard her footfall and picked up a newspaper off his desk and handed it to her with an unreadable expression. 'The press have identified you as my new mistress.'

She took the paper and looked at the photo of her, standing on the deck of his boat with Alessandra asleep against her shoulder. The caption read: *New stepmother for tragic toddler heiress Alessandra Valente? London primary schoolteacher Eliza Lincoln has been identified as the mystery woman in Leo Valente's life.*

Eliza swallowed thickly. What if Samantha saw this? Would it hit the press back in Britain? What would Samantha think of her? She had told her a version of the truth rather than tell her an outright lie. She'd said she was visiting an old friend in Italy to fill in for the regular nanny who was taking a little break. She hadn't said the old friend was actually the man she had met and fallen in love with four years ago. Now it would be splashed over every newspaper in the country that she had gone off and had a clandestine affair. Samantha would be so dreadfully hurt. She would feel *so* betrayed.

'You might want to warn your fiancé in case this gets picked up by the British tabloids,' Leo said as if he had read her thoughts.

She chewed at her lower lip. 'Yes…'

'I suspect there will be quite a lot of press attention when we arrive in London,' he said. 'It will blow over after a day or two. Remember you are forbidden to comment on anything to do with your time with us here.'

Eliza straightened her shoulders as she handed him back the paper. 'I haven't forgotten.'

The flight to London went without a hitch but, as Leo had predicted, there was a cluster of photographers waiting outside for a glimpse of the young Englishwoman who had been spotted on his boat with his little girl the day before. The click, click, click of camera shutters going off sounded like a heavy round of bullets being discharged.

'Miss Lincoln, what does your fiancé Ewan Brockman think of you spending the last couple of weeks with billionaire Leo Valente in his luxury villa on the Amalfi coast in Italy?'

Eliza totally froze. How on earth did these people find out this stuff? What else did they know? For all these years Samantha had been adamant Ewan's condition should be kept out of the press. She had done everything she could to keep Ewan's dignity intact and Eliza had loved and respected her for it. Who had released his name? Someone at school? Only Georgie knew of the extent of Ewan's condition. Had a journalist pressed her for details? That was another phone call Eliza should have made. She should have warned Georgie to keep quiet if anyone approached her to comment on her private life.

'Miss Lincoln is my daughter's fill-in nanny,' Leo said before Eliza could get her mouth to work. 'She will be returning to her fiancé in a matter of days. Please give us room. My daughter is becoming upset.'

It was true—Alessandra was starting to whimper in distress, but Eliza had a feeling it had more to do with Leo's statement that she was leaving them to go back to her old life rather than the surge of the press. She cuddled the little girl close to her chest and, keeping her head down against the flashing cameras, she walked into the hotel with Leo until they were finally safe in their suite.

It didn't take long to settle Alessandra, who was tired after the journey. Marella, who had travelled with them, offered to babysit while Leo and Eliza went out for a meal.

'Are you sure this is wise?' Eliza asked as Leo closed his phone after booking a table at a restaurant.

'We need to eat, don't we?'

'Yes, but surely a meal in our suite would be perfectly fine?' She fiddled with the chain around her neck with agitated fingers. 'What's the point in deliberately entering the fray? They'll just hound us all over again.'

He gave her an ironic lift of his brow. 'You were the one who said I shouldn't hide Alessandra away.'

'We're not talking about Alessandra,' she said stiffly. 'We're talking about me, about *my* reputation. People are going to get hurt by all that stuff they're saying about me.'

'I take it you mean your fiancé?' His eyes were hard as stone as they held hers.

Eliza still hadn't had either the time or the privacy to call Samantha. Any moment now she expected her phone to ring, with Samantha asking her what the hell was going on. It was making her nervy and jumpy. A headache was pounding at her temples and a pit of nausea was corroding the lining of her stomach like flesh-eating acid. 'I don't like being called your mistress.'

'It's the truth, isn't it?'

'Not for much longer.' She scooped up her bag and

slung it over her shoulder. 'Let's get this over with. I want to get back as quickly as possible and go to bed.'

He gave her a smouldering look as he held the door open for her. 'I couldn't have put it better myself.'

They were halfway through dinner at an exclusive restaurant in Mayfair when Eliza's phone audibly vibrated from inside her bag. She had set it to silent but hadn't thought to turn off the vibration and illumination component. She tried to ignore it, hoping that Leo hadn't heard, but the glow every time it vibrated was visible through the top of her bag.

'Aren't you going to answer it?' he asked.

'Um…it can wait.' She picked up her glass of wine and took a little sip to settle her nerves.

The phone vibrated again.

'Sounds like someone really wants to talk to you,' he said.

Eliza knew it was pathetic of her to keep putting off the inevitable. It was a lifetime habit of hers to procrastinate, hoping that things would go away or be resolved on their own, but it was only prolonging the agony. Wasn't that why she was in this mess? She should have been honest right from the word go with Ewan. She shouldn't have waited for months and months without saying anything, letting him believe everything was fine when it wasn't. Hadn't she learned her lesson by now? She had to face things, not hide from them. 'Um… will you excuse me?' She rose to her feet. 'I won't be long.'

There was no one in the lipstick lounge adjacent to the restroom, so Eliza sat on a chintz-covered chair and pressed Samantha's number. 'Hi, it's me.'

'Oh, darling,' Samantha said with an audible sigh

of relief. 'I'm so glad you called back so quickly. I'm bringing Ewan up to London to see the specialist tomorrow. You know how we've been on that waiting list for months and months? Well, there's been a sudden cancellation. I know you're probably tied up with your little nanny job, but I was hoping since you're back in London for a couple of days that you could come with me. Do you think you could get an hour or two off? You know how hard I find managing him all by myself. I called the agency and asked for a respite carer to come with me but there's no one available at such short notice. I was just hoping you could come with us. I know it's a lot to ask.'

Eliza felt her insides twist into cripplingly tight knots of guilt. How could she say no? She knew it wasn't the physical support with Ewan that Samantha was after. She knew how much hope Samantha had invested in seeing this particular specialist. She also knew Samantha was going to be completely shattered when the specialist gave her the same prognosis every other specialist she had taken Ewan to had done.

How could she let her face that all by herself?

Leo would be tied up with his work most of the day as well as his meeting with the bursar so it shouldn't cause too much of a problem. Marella probably wouldn't mind giving her a couple of hours. She needn't even ask Leo's permission. He would probably say no in any case. He would probably assume she was going against his orders and sneaking in a passionate session with her fiancé.

If only he knew…

'Of course I'll come with you,' she said. 'Text me the address and the time and I'll be there.'

'You're an angel,' Samantha said. 'I honestly don't know what I'd do without you.'

Eliza took an uneven breath and slowly released it. 'I thought you were calling about the stuff in the press… I guess you've seen it by now, otherwise you wouldn't have known I was here. I should have called you first to warn you. I'm sorry. It all sounds so horribly sordid.'

'Oh, sweetie, don't worry about that,' Samantha said. 'I know what the press are like. They make up stuff all the time. You can't believe a word you read these days. It's just pure sensationalism. I know you would never leave Ewan.'

Eliza felt guilt come down on her like a tower of bricks. *But I had left him!* The words were jammed in her throat, stuck behind a wall of strangling emotion.

'See you tomorrow, darling,' Samantha said. 'Love you.'

'Love you, too.' Eliza gave a long, heavy sigh as she switched the phone off. And, taking a deep breath, she got to her feet and walked back to where Leo was waiting for her.

He stood up when she came back to the table. 'Is everything all right?'

Eliza gave him a brief forced smile as she sat down. 'Of course.' She picked up her wine glass and cradled it in both hands to keep them occupied.

'Who was it?'

'Just a friend.'

'Eliza.'

She brought up her gaze and her chin. 'Yes?'

'I don't need to remind you of the rules, do I?'

'Would you like to screen all my calls while you're at it?' She put her glass down with a little clunk. 'Or how about you scroll through my emails and texts?'

He frowned and reached for his own wine glass. 'I'm sorry. I don't want to spoil our truce.'

'Truce? Is that what you call this?' She waved a hand to encompass the romantic setting.

'Look, I don't want to spend the only time we have alone together arguing. That wasn't the point of going out to dinner this evening.'

'What *is* the point?' Was it to make her fall in love with him again and then drop her cold? Was it to make her feel even more wretched about her other life once this was over?

He took one of her tightly clenched hands and began to massage her stiff fingers until they softened and relaxed. 'The point is to get to know one another better,' he said. 'I've noticed we either have mad, passionate sex or argue like fiends when we are alone. I want to try doing something different for a change.'

Eliza looked at her hand in his, the way his olive skin was so much of a contrast to her creamy one. She felt the stirring of her body the longer he held her. Those fingers had touched every part of her body. They could make her sizzle with excitement just by looking at them. It was becoming harder and harder to keep her emotions hidden away. She wasn't supposed to be falling in love with him again. She wasn't supposed to be dreaming of a life with him.

That was not an option for her.

She raised her gaze back to meet his. 'What did you have in mind?'

He smiled a slow smile that made his eyes become soft and warm, and another lock on her heart loosened. 'Why don't you wait and see?'

An hour later they were on a dance floor, not in an exclusive nightclub or a hotel ballroom, but on the balcony of their hotel suite. Champagne was in an ice bucket, romantic music was playing from the sound system and the vista of the city of London was spread out below them in a glittering array of twinkling lights and famous landmarks.

Eliza was in Leo's arms, dancing like Cinderella at the ball. The clock had moved way past midnight but this was one night she didn't want to end. She had never considered herself a particularly good dancer but somehow in Leo's arms she felt as if she was floating across the balcony, their bodies at one and their footwork perfectly in tune, apart from a couple of early missteps on her part.

She leaned her head against his chest and breathed in the warm citrus and clean male scent of him. 'This is nice...'

His hand pressed against the small of her back to bring her closer. 'Where did you learn to dance?' he asked.

She looked up at him with a rueful smile. 'I know, I'm rubbish at it, aren't I? I've probably mashed your toes to a pulp.'

He gave a deep chuckle and kissed her forehead. 'Don't worry. I can still walk.'

Eliza laid her head back down against his chest as she thought of Ewan sitting in that chair, his legs and arms useless, his once brilliant brain now in scattered fragments that could no longer connect.

The line of that old nursery rhyme played inside her head, as it had done so many times over the last five and a half years: *All the King's horses and all the King's men couldn't put Humpty Dumpty together again...*

CHAPTER THIRTEEN

THE NEXT DAY, Leo got back earlier than he'd expected from his meetings. He had particularly enjoyed the one with the community school bursar. He had made a commitment to the school and he couldn't wait to tell Eliza about it. The project she had set her heart on would go ahead, no matter how things turned out when her time with him was up.

Last night he had sensed a shift in their relationship. In the past they had had sex, last night they had made love. He had felt the difference in her kisses and caresses. He wondered if she had sensed the difference in his.

Did it mean she might reconsider her engagement? He had done a quick Internet search on her fiancé but he hadn't uncovered much at all. It surprised him for in this day and age just about everyone had a social media page or blog or website. Was the man some sort of recluse? It had niggled at him all day. After what had come out in the papers yesterday, why hadn't the guy stormed into the hotel and punched Leo's lights out? It didn't make sense. If Ewan Brockman loved Eliza, then surely he would have come forward and demanded an explanation.

It was time to have a no holds barred conversation

with her. Something wasn't quite adding up and he wasn't going to stop digging until he found out what it was—and there was no time like the present.

Leo came into the suite to find Marella sitting on the sofa with a book while Alessandra was having a nap in the next room.

'Where's Eliza?' he asked as he put his briefcase down.

'She went to do a bit of shopping,' Marella said, closing the book and putting it to one side. 'She's only been gone a couple of hours. I told her to take all the time she wanted. She should be back soon. Why don't you call her and meet her for a drink? I'll give Alessandra her bath and supper.'

'Good idea.' He gave her an appreciative smile and reached for his phone. He frowned as the call went through to message bank. He sent her a text but there was no response.

'She's probably turned her phone off,' Marella said.

'Did she say where she was intending to shop?'

Marella pursed her lips for a moment. 'I think she said something about going to Queen Square.'

He frowned as he put his phone back in his pocket. Queen Square was where the world-renowned UCL Institute of Neurology was situated. He'd driven past it a couple of times on previous trips to London. Great Ormond Street Hospital was close by. Why was Eliza going there? Sure, there were plenty of shops in the Bloomsbury district, but why had she told Marella she was going to Queen Square of all places?

Leo saw her from half a block away. She was standing talking with an older woman in her fifties outside the UCL Institute of Neurology. The older woman looked very distressed. She kept mopping at her eyes with a scrunched up tissue. Eliza was holding the hand of a gaunt young man in his late twenties who was strapped in a wheelchair, complete with breathing apparatus and a urinary catheter that was just visible under the tartan blanket that covered his thin, muscle-wasted legs.

Leo felt as if someone had thrown a ninety-pound dumb-bell straight at his chest.

Her fiancé.

He swallowed against a monkey wrench of guilt that was stuck sideways in his throat. Her fiancé was a quadriplegic. The poor man was totally and utterly incapacitated. He didn't even seem to be aware of where he was or whom he was with; he was staring vacantly into space. Leo watched as Eliza gently wiped some drool from the side of the young man's mouth with a tissue.

Oh, dear God, what had he done?

Why hadn't she told him?

Why the hell hadn't she told him?

He didn't know whether to be furious at her or to feel sorry for her. Why let him think the very worst of her for all this time? It all made horrible sense now that he had seen her fiancé with his very own eyes. It wasn't a normal relationship. How could it be, with that poor young man sitting drooling and slumped in his chair like that? Was that why she had taken the money he had offered her? She had done it for her fiancé.

His gut churned and roiled with remorse.

He had exploited her in the worst way imaginable.

Leo turned back the way he had come. He needed time to think about this—to get his head around it all. He didn't want to have it out with her on the street with her fiancé and his mother—he assumed it was his mother—watching on. He took a couple of deep calming breaths but they caught on the claws of his guilt that were still tearing at his throat.

Eliza had turned down his marriage proposal because she had honoured her commitment to her fiancé. It took the promise of *in sickness and in health* to a whole new level. She hadn't done it because she hadn't loved *him*. His instincts back then had been right after all. He had felt sure she had fallen in love with him. He had felt sure of it last night when she had danced in his arms on the balcony and made love with him with such exquisite tenderness.

He had felt his own feelings for her stirring beneath the concrete slab of his denial where he had buried them four years ago.

He thought back to all the little clues she had dropped about her fiancé. If only he had pushed a little harder he might have got her to trust him enough to tell him before things had gone this far. Was it too late to undo the damage? Would she forgive him?

His heart felt as if someone had slammed it with a sledgehammer.

What did it matter if she did or not? She was still tied to her fiancé. She still wore his ring, if not on her finger then around her neck.

Close to her heart...

Eliza got back to the hotel a little flustered at being later than she'd planned. Samantha had taken the news hard, as she had expected. There was no magical cure for Ewan. No special treatment or miraculous therapy that would make his body and mind function again. It was heartbreaking to think of Samantha's hopes being dashed all over again. What mother didn't want the best for her child? Wasn't Leo the same with Alessandra?

He would move heaven and earth to give his little girl a cure for her blindness, but it wasn't to be.

Samantha had been so upset Eliza had found herself promising to spend the rest of the summer break with her and Ewan once she got back from Italy. Even as the words had come out of her mouth she had wished she could pull them back. She felt as if she was being torn in two. Leaving Leo for the second time would be hard enough, but this time she would be leaving Alessandra as well.

Could life get any more viciously cruel?

Eliza opened the door of the suite and Leo turned to face her from where he was standing at the window overlooking the view. Her heart gave a little jolt in her chest. She had hoped to get back before he did. 'I'm sorry I'm late…' She put her handbag down and put a hand to her hair to smooth it back from where the breeze had teased it loose. 'The shops were crazily busy.'

His eyes went to her empty hands. 'Not a very successful trip, I take it?'

Her heart gave another lurch. 'No…no, it wasn't…' She tried to smile but somehow her mouth wouldn't cooperate. 'Where's Alessandra?'

'With Marella in the suite next door.'

'I hope you didn't mind me having a bit of time to myself.' She couldn't quite hold his gaze.

'I seem to remember telling you before that you are not under lock and key.' He wandered over to the bar area of the suite. 'Would you like a drink?'

'Um…yes, thank you.'

He handed her a glass of chilled white wine. 'Shopping is such thirsty work, *sì*?'

Eliza still couldn't read his inscrutable expression.

'Yes…' She took a sip of her drink. 'How did your meeting with the bursar go?'

'I've decided to bankroll your project.'

She blinked at him. 'You…you have?'

'I read your proposal in detail.' His expression remained masklike. 'There are a few loose ends that need tying up, but I think it won't take too much time to sort them out.'

Eliza forced her tense shoulders to relax. Was there some sort of subtext to this conversation or was she just imagining it? It was hard to gauge his mood. He seemed as if he was waiting for her to say something, or was she imagining that too? 'I can't thank you enough for what you're doing. I'm not sure why you're doing it.'

'You can't guess?'

She flicked over her dry lips with her tongue. 'I'm not foolish enough to think it's because you care something for me. You've made it pretty clear from the outset that you don't.' *Apart from last night, when it had seemed as if he was making love with her for the very first time.*

There was a silence that seemed to have a disturbing undercurrent to it. It stretched and stretched like a too thin wire being pulled by industrial strength strainers.

'Why didn't you tell me?' Leo asked.

'Tell you what?'

He let out a stiff curse that made her flinch. 'Let's stop playing games. I saw you today.'

Her stomach clenched. 'Saw me where?'

'With your fiancé. I assume that's who the young man in the wheelchair is?'

'Yes…'

His frown was so deep it joined his eyebrows like a bridge over his eyes. 'Is that all you can say?'

Eliza put her glass down before she dropped it. 'I was going to tell you.' She hugged her arms across her body. 'I would've told you days ago but you forbade me to even speak his name out loud.'

'That is not a good enough excuse and you know it.' He glared at her, but whether it was with anger or frustration she couldn't quite tell. 'You could've insisted I listen. You could've told me the first day I came to see you. For God's sake, you could've told me the first night we met. And you damn well *should've* told me the night I proposed to you.'

'Why?' She tossed him a glare right on back. 'What difference would it have made?'

'How can you *ask* that?' His tone was incredulous. 'I wanted to marry you. I still want to marry you.'

Eliza noticed he hadn't said he loved her. He just wanted a wife and a stepmother for his daughter. Wasn't that what the press had said? 'I'm not free to marry you.'

He came over and put his hands on her shoulders. 'Listen to me, Eliza. We can sort this out. Your fiancé will understand. You just have to tell him you want to be with someone else.'

She pulled out of his hold and put some distance between them, her arms going across her middle again. 'It's not that simple…' She took a breath that tore at her throat like talons. 'It's my fault he's in that chair.'

'What do you mean?'

She looked at him again. 'I ended our relationship. He left my flat upset—devastated, actually. He was in no fit state to drive. I should never have let him go. It was my fault. If I hadn't broken our engagement that night he would still be a healthy, active, intelligent, fully functioning man.' She choked back a sob. 'I can't even tell him I'm sorry. He doesn't have any understanding of language any more. He's little more than a body in a chair. He can't even breathe on his own. How can I tell his mother I want to be with someone else after what I've done to her son?'

'You didn't tell her you'd broken off the engagement?' Leo asked with a puzzled frown.

Eliza shook her head. 'When I got the call, she was already at the hospital. She was shattered by what the doctors had told her about his condition. He wasn't expected to make it through the night. How could I tell her then?'

'What about later?'

'I couldn't…' She took another shaky breath. 'How could I? She would think—like everyone else would—that I was trying to weasel my way out of a life of looking after him. It would be such a cruel and selfish and heartless thing to do.'

'Aren't you being a little hard on yourself? Would you have expected him to give up his life if you had been the one injured?'

Eliza had thought about it but had always come up with the same answer. 'No, because he would never have broken up with me without warning. He would have prepared me for it, like I should've done for him. We'd been together since I was sixteen. It was wrong of me to dump it on him like that. He loved me so much. And look at what that love has cost him. It's only fair that I give up my future for him. I owe him that.'

'You don't owe him your future,' Leo said. 'Come on, Eliza, you're not thinking rationally. His mother wouldn't want you to give up your life like this. Surely she's told you to move on with your life?'

Eliza gave him a despairing look. 'I'm all she has left. She lost his father when Ewan was a little boy. Now she's as good as lost him, too. How can I walk away from her now? I'm like a daughter to her and she's been like a mother to me. I can't do it. I just can't.'

'What if I talk to her? I'll make her understand how it's unfair of her to expect so much of you.'

Eliza shook her head sadly. 'You're so used to getting whatever you want, but sometimes there are things you just can't have, no matter how hard and desperately you wish for them.'

'Do you think I don't know that?' he asked. 'I have a child I would do anything on this earth to help.'

'I know you would and that's exactly what Samantha is like. She's a wonderful mother and a wonderful person. It would devastate her if I was to go away and live with you in Italy.'

'What if we moved to London? I could work from here. It would be a big adjustment but I could do it. There are good schools for the blind here. Alessandra will soon adjust.'

Eliza pulled her emotions back into line like a ball of loose yarn being wound up rapidly and tightly. 'I can't marry you, Leo. You have to accept that. Once the month is up I have to come back to my life here. I've already promised Samantha to spend the last couple of weeks of the holidays with her and Ewan.'

'You *do* have a choice. Damn it, Eliza, can't you see that? You're locking yourself away out of guilt. It's not going to help anyone, least of all your fiancé.' He sent his hand through his hair again. 'I suppose that's why you took the money. It was for him, wasn't it?'

'Yes…'

'Why didn't you ask for more?'

'I was uncomfortable enough as it was, without exploiting your offer.'

He gave an embittered laugh. 'Let's say it how it was. It wasn't an offer. I blackmailed you. I can never forgive myself for that.' He moved to the other side of the room as if he needed the distance from her to think.

'I'm sorry…' Eliza broke the silence. 'I've handled this so badly. I've made it so much worse.' She took a deep shuddering breath as she finally came to a decision. 'I'm not going to go back with you to Italy tomorrow. It wouldn't be fair to Alessandra. It will make it so much harder when the month is up.'

He swung around to glare at her. 'What…you're just going to walk away? What about the contract you signed? Are you forgetting the terms and conditions?'

'If you decide to act on them, then I'll have to face that if and when it happens.'

'I'll withdraw my offer for your project. I'll tell the bursar I've changed my mind.' His jaw was clenched tight, his eyes flashing at her furiously.

Eliza knew it was risky calling his bluff but she hoped he would come to understand this was the best way to handle things—the cleanest way. 'Will you say goodbye to Alessandra for me? I don't want to wake her now. It will only upset her more.'

His look was scathing. 'I never took you for a coward.'

'It has to be this way.'

'Why does it?' His eyes flashed at her again. 'Are you really going to stand there and deny that you love me?'

Eliza steeled herself as she held his gaze. 'I have never said I loved you.'

A muscle flicked in his cheek and his eyes hardened. 'So it was always just about the money.'

'Yes.'

His lip curled mockingly. 'And the sex.'

She gave him her best worldly look. 'That too.'

He sucked in a breath and moved to the window overlooking the leafy street below. 'I'll have Marella send your things to you when we get back.'

'Thank you.' Eliza moved past to collect her things from the suite.

'I won't say goodbye,' he said. 'I think we've both said all that needs to be said.'

Except I love you, Eliza thought sadly as she softly closed the door as she left.

CHAPTER FOURTEEN

ELIZA SPENT THE first week with Samantha and Ewan in Suffolk in a state of emotional distress so acute it made her feel physically ill. She couldn't sleep and she could barely get a morsel of food past her lips. Every time she thought of Leo or Alessandra her chest would ache as if a stack of heavy books was balanced on it. But she had no choice but to keep what she was feeling to herself as Samantha was still dealing with her heartbreak over the hopelessness of Ewan's situation.

But towards the middle of the second week Samantha seemed to pick herself up. She had even been out a couple of times in the evening while Eliza sat with Ewan. She hadn't said where she was going or whom she was going with and Eliza hadn't asked. But each time Samantha returned she looked a little less strained and unhappy.

'Darling, you don't seem yourself since you came back from the nanny job,' Samantha said as she watched Eliza push the food around her plate during dinner. 'Is everything all right? Are you missing the little girl? She's rather a cute little button, isn't she?'

'Yes, she is. And yes, I do miss her.'

'What a pity she's blind.' Samantha picked up her

glass of lemonade. 'But that's not the worst thing that can happen to a person, is it?'

'No…it isn't.'

'I would've loved a daughter,' Samantha said. 'Don't get me wrong—I loved having a son. No mother could have asked for a better one than Ewan. And I've been so fortunate in having you as a surrogate daughter. I can't thank you enough for always being there for me and for Ewan.'

Eliza put her cutlery down and gripped her hands together on her lap underneath the table. It had been brewing inside her for days, this pressing need to put things straight at last. She could no longer live with this terrible guilt. She wanted to move on with her life. She could no longer deny her love for Leo. Even if he didn't love her, surely she owed him the truth of her feelings. 'Samantha…there's something you need to know about that night…I know it will be hard for you to hear and I don't blame you for thinking I'm just making it up to get out of this situation, but it's my fault Ewan had the accident that night.'

The silence was long and painful.

'I broke off our engagement,' Eliza continued. 'Ewan left my place so upset he should never have got behind the wheel of that car. I should never have let him leave like that. I'd bottled up my feelings for so long and then that night I just couldn't hold it in any longer. I told him I didn't love him any more. He was devastated.' She choked back a sob. 'I know you can't possibly forgive me. I will never forgive myself. But I want to have a life now. I want to be with Leo and his little girl. I love him. I'm sorry if that upsets you or you think it's selfish but I can't live this lie any more. I feel so wicked to have accepted the love you've given so freely and so generously when all this time I've been lying to you.'

Samantha let out a deep uneven sigh. She suddenly looked much older than her years. She seemed to sag in the chair as if her bones had got tired of staying neatly aligned. 'I suppose it's only right that you lied to me.'

'What do you mean?'

Samantha gave her a pained look. 'I've been lying to you too for the last few years.'

'I don't understand…' Eliza frowned in puzzlement. 'What do you mean? How have *you* lied to me? I'm the one who covered up what happened that night. I should have told you at the hospital. I should have told you well before this.'

Samantha took a deep breath and released it in a jagged stream. 'He told me.'

Eliza was still frowning in confusion. 'Who told you what?'

'Ewan.' Samantha met her gaze levelly. 'He told me you'd broken up with him.'

Eliza felt her heart slam against her ribcage as if it had hit a brick wall at high speed. 'When did he tell you?'

Samantha's throat moved up and down like a mouse moving under a rug. 'I called him just a minute or two after he'd left your place.' Her face crumpled. 'I'm so sorry. I should've told you before now. I've been feeling so wretchedly guilty. It was my fault. I was on the phone to him just moments before he crashed into that tree.' She gave a ragged sob and dropped her head into her hands. 'He told me you'd ended your engagement. He was upset. I told him to pull himself together. I was furious with him for being so surprised by your ending things. I'd seen it coming for months. He was livid. I'd never heard him so angry. He hung up on me. It was my fault. I caused his accident.'

'No.' Eliza rushed over to wrap her arms around Samantha. 'No, please don't blame yourself.'

'I knew you were unhappy,' Samantha sobbed into her shoulder. 'I knew it but I didn't say anything to him or to you. I wanted it to all work out. I wanted you to be the daughter I'd always longed for. I wanted us to be a family. That's all I wanted.'

Eliza closed her eyes as she held Samantha tightly in her arms. 'You're not to blame. You're not in any way to blame. I'm still that daughter. I'll always be that daughter and part of your family.'

Samantha pulled back to look at her. 'There's something else I want to confess.'

'What is it?'

'I've met someone.' She blushed like a teenager confessing to her first crush. 'He's a doctor at the clinic I take Ewan to. He's been wonderfully supportive. We've been on a few dates. That's where I've been going the last couple of nights. It's happened very quickly but we have such a lot in common. He has a daughter with cerebral palsy. I think he's going to ask me to marry him. If he does, I've decided I'll say yes.'

Eliza smiled with genuine happiness. 'But that's wonderful! You deserve to be happy.'

Samantha gave her a tremulous smile. 'I've been so worried about telling you, but when I saw all that fuss in the press about you and Leo Valente, I started to wonder if it might finally be time for both of us to move on with our lives.'

Eliza blinked back tears. 'I'm not sure if I have a future with Leo, but I want to tell him I love him. I think I owe him that.'

Samantha grasped her hands in hers. 'You must tell him how you feel. You don't owe Ewan anything. He is happy, or at least as happy as he can ever be. He's not aware of anything other than his immediate physical comfort. Robert has explained all that to me. It's helped me come to terms with it all. Ewan is not the same person now. He can never be that person again. But he's happy. And you and I need to be happy for him. Will you promise me that?'

'I will be happy for you and for Ewan. I promise you.' Eliza took off the chain from around her neck and handed Samantha the engagement ring. 'I think you're going to need this.'

Samantha clutched it tightly in her hand and smiled. 'You know something? I think you might be right.'

Eliza arrived at Leo's villa at three in the afternoon. Marella answered the door and immediately swept her up in a bone-crushing hug. 'I knew you'd come back. I told Signor Valente and Alessandra you'd be back. They've been so miserable. Like a bad English summer, *sì*?'

Eliza smiled in spite of the turmoil of her emotions. 'Where is he? I should've phoned first to see if he was at home. I didn't think…I just wanted to get here and talk to him as soon as I could.'

'He's not here,' Marella said. 'But he's not far away. He's at the old villa.'

'The one he had four years ago?'

'Sì,' Marella nodded. 'He thinks it would be better for Alessandra. I agree with him. This place is too big for her.'

Eliza felt her heart lift. 'Is she here?'

'She is sleeping upstairs. Do you want to see her?'

'I'd love to see her, but I think I'd better talk to Leo first.'

Marella beamed. 'I think that is a very good idea.'

Eliza pushed open the squeaky old wrought iron gate of the villa that was tucked into one of the hillsides that overlooked the stunning views of the coast below. The garden was very neglected and the villa needed a coat of paint but it was like stepping back in time. The scent of lemon blossom was tangy in the air. The cobblestones underneath the thin soles of her ballet flats were warm from a full day of sun. The birds were twittering in the trees and shrubbery nearby, just as they had four years ago.

She walked up the path to the front door but before she could reach up to use the rusty old knocker the door opened. Leo looked as if he had just encountered a ghost. He stared down at her, his throat moving up and down as if he couldn't quite get his voice to work.

Eliza dropped her hand back down by her side. 'I came to offer my services as a nanny but it looks to me that what you really need is a gardener and a painter.'

'I already have a nanny.' His expression was difficult to read but she thought she saw a glint in those dark eyes.

'Do you have any other positions vacant?' Eliza asked.

'Which position did you have in mind?'

She gave a little shrug of her shoulder. 'Lover, confidante, stepmother, wife—that sort of thing. I'm pretty flexible.'

A tiny half smile tugged at the edges of his mouth. 'Do you want a temporary post or are you thinking about something a little more long-term?'

Eliza put her hands on his chest, splaying the fingers of her right hand so she could feel the steady beat of his heart. 'I'm thinking in terms of forever.'

'What makes you think I'd offer you forever?'

She searched his features for a moment. Had she got it wrong? Had she jumped to the wrong conclusion? 'You do love me, don't you? I know you haven't said it but nor have I. And I do. I love you so much. I've always loved you. From the moment I met you I felt you were the only person for me.'

He put his arms around her. 'Of course I love you. How can you doubt that?'

She tiptoed her other hand up to the stubbly growth on his jaw. 'I've put you through hell and yet you still love me.'

He cupped her face in his hands. 'Isn't that what true love is supposed to do? Conquer everything in its path and triumph over all in the end?'

'I didn't know it was possible to love someone so much.'

'A couple of weeks ago you walked out of my life and I didn't think you'd be back. It was like four years ago all over again. What's changed?'

'*I've* changed,' she said. 'I've finally realised that life dishes up what it dishes up and we all have to deal with it in our own way and in our own time. I will probably always feel sad and guilty about Ewan. I can't change that. It's just what is. But I'm not making his life any better or worse by denying myself a chance at happiness. He would want me to live his life for him. I'm going to do my very best to do that. And my new life starts now, here with you and Alessandra. You are my family, but I have to say I need to keep a special corner open for Samantha. She's the most amazing surrogate mother in the world and I don't want to lose her.'

Leo put his arms around her and hugged her tightly. 'Then you won't,' he said. 'I need a mother, too, and Alessandra desperately needs a hands-on grandmother. Do you think she would have enough love to stretch to us as well?'

Eliza smiled as she hugged him tight. 'I'm absolutely sure of it.'

* * * * *

SPECIAL EXCERPT FROM

Presents

USA TODAY *bestselling author Lucy Monroe brings you a passionate new duet,* BY HIS ROYAL DECREE, *from Harlequin® Presents®, starting with ONE NIGHT HEIR in July 2013.*

* * *

"I will not leave you again." It was a vow, accompanied by the slipping of the ring onto her finger.

Even though it was prompted by her pregnancy and the fact she now carried the heir to the Volyarus throne, the promise in his voice poured over the jagged edges of her heart with soothing warmth. The small weight of the metal band and diamonds on her finger was a source of more comfort than she would ever have believed possible.

She was not sure her heart would ever be whole again, but it did not have to hurt like it had for ten weeks.

"I won't leave you, either."

"I know." A small sound, almost a sigh, escaped his mouth. "Now we must convince your body that it still belongs to me."

"You have a very possessive side."

"This is nothing new."

"Actually, it kind of is." He'd shown indications of a possessive nature when they were dating, but he'd never been so primal about it before. "You're like a caveman."

His smile was predatory, his eyes burning with sensual intent. "You carry my child. It makes me feel *very* possessive, takes me back to the responses of my ancestors."

HPEXP0613-1

Air escaped her lungs in an unexpected whoosh. "Oh."

"I have read that some pregnant women desire sex more often than usual."

"I…" She wasn't sure what she felt in that department right now.

She always seemed to want him and could not imagine her hormones increasing that all too visceral need.

"However, I had not realized the pregnancy could impact the father in the same way." There was no mistaking his meaning.

Maks wanted her. And not in some casual, sex-as-physical-exercise way. The expression in his dark eyes said he wanted to devour her, the mother of his child, sexually.

Gillian shivered in response to that look.

"Cold?" he purred, pushing even closer. "Let me warm you."

"I'm not co—" But she wasn't allowed to finish the thought.

His mouth covered hers in a kiss that demanded full submission and reciprocation.

* * *

Find out what happens when this powerful prince raises the stakes of their marriage of convenience in ONE NIGHT HEIR, out July 2013!

And don't miss the explosive second story, PRINCE OF SECRETS, available August 2013.

HPEXP0613-1

COMING NEXT MONTH from Harlequin Presents®

AVAILABLE JUNE 18, 2013

#3153 HIS MOST EXQUISITE CONQUEST

The Legendary Finn Brothers

Emma Darcy

The vivacious Lucy Flippence has fallen prey to Michael Finn, whose reputation is legendary. She might be only a tick on his to-do list, but even the luxury lifestyle can't mask the feelings her secret has forced her to hide....

#3154 A SHADOW OF GUILT

Sicily's Corretti Dynasty

Abby Green

Valentina has always blamed Gio Corretti for her brother's death. But when she needs help, there's only one man she can turn to—the cold, inscrutable Gio, whose green eyes flash with guilt, regret and a passion that calls to her.

#3155 ONE NIGHT HEIR

By His Royal Decree

Lucy Monroe

Duty comes before desire for Prince Maksim. He knew that when he cut his ties to his mistress Gillian Harris. But when she gets pregnant this fierce royal Cossack must claim his heir and convince her to be his queen!

#3156 HIS BRAND OF PASSION

The Bryants: Powerful & Proud

Kate Hewitt

For billionaire Aaron Bryant, money usually solves everything, but he's not had a problem like this before. One unbridled night of passion with sassy Zoe Parker has left two little lines on a test—turning both their lives upside down.

#3157 THE COUPLE WHO FOOLED THE WORLD
Maisey Yates

Most women would kill to be on Ferro Calvaresi's arm. But Julia Anderson is not most women. When a major deal requires these two rivals to play nicely...*together*...is the world's hottest new couple beginning to believe their own lie?

#3158 THE RETURN OF HER PAST
Lindsay Armstrong

Housekeeper's daughter Mia Gardiner knew her feelings for multimillionaire Carlos O'Connor were foolish. Until she caught the ruthless playboy's eye. Even now, older and wiser, Mia has never forgotten the feel of his touch. Then, like a whirlwind, Carlos returns....

#3159 IN PETRAKIS'S POWER
Maggie Cox

To safeguard her family's future, Natalie makes a deal with the devil—Ludo Petrakis. She must travel to Greece—as his fiancée! But seeing the cracks in Ludo's unshakable control, she finds that it gets harder to resist the smoldering tension between them....

#3160 PROOF OF THEIR SIN
One Night with Consequences
Dani Collins

Lauren is pregnant and marriage is the only way to avoid scandal, but she still bears the scars from the first time she said "I do." Can she trust the powerful but guarded Paolo enough to reveal the truth?

HPCNM0613RB